The Dark Truth

With best wishes
Ellen Harding

The Dark Truth

A Crystal Legacy

Ellen Hardwick

Matador
9 Priory Business Park,
Wistow Road, Kibworth Beauchamp,
Leicestershire. LE8 0RX
Tel: (+44) 116 279 2299
Fax: (+44) 116 279 2277
Email: books@troubador.co.uk
Web: www.troubador.co.uk/matador

ISBN 978 1784621 483

British Library Cataloguing in Publication Data.
A catalogue record for this book is available from the British Library.

Typeset by Troubador Publishing Ltd, Leicester, UK
Printed and bound by CPI Group (UK) Ltd, Croydon, CR0 4YY

Matador is an imprint of Troubador Publishing Ltd

MIX
Paper from responsible sources
FSC® C013604

Other books by the author

Untold Truth

The first book of this trilogy.

A spiritual mystery which takes Jane and Mark on a journey that transforms their lives when they discover their untold truth.

The Dark Truth – A Crystal Legacy

The second book of this trilogy.

It follows Jane and Mark's journey where Mark's secret and past is revealed when something happens to the earth's crystals.

The Ultimate Truth – The power of One

The last book of this trilogy.

Jane and Mark's journey comes to a final conclusion when Mark's steps into his power.

Out soon – check author's page for details
www.ellenhardwick.wordpress.com
www.troubador.co.uk/book_info.asp?bookid=1951

CHAPTER ONE

Fiona saw the tall, lanky, sharp-faced man hovering over her office desk and knew instantly she didn't like him. As she approached, he turned to look at her and it felt like his shifty eyes were scanning every inch of her body. He moved to the front of her desk when she sat in the chair.

'Can I help you?' she said firmly.

'Well darling, I'm looking for someone who I believe may work here.'

The overly-done, smooth-toned voice and the use of the word "darling" irritated her. She didn't trust him one bit.

'Who did you say you worked for?'

'I didn't. It's confidential.' He showed her a card.

'You're a private investigator eh? Well there is nothing to investigate here.'

'Common love, it wouldn't hurt you to take a look at this photo.' He shoved the picture in front of her face. It was of a man with long, blond hair who was clean-shaven and slightly overweight.

'Never seen him before.'

'Perhaps he's dating someone who works here?' he said, smiling and leaning slightly towards her.

Fiona edged back her chair. 'Nope I don't think so. I know most of the girls' boyfriends and he's not one of them.'

The man straightened sharply and his voice hardened.

'So who sits in this office?' He pointed to the adjoining room.

The sign on the door clearly stated, Jane Fairway.

Fiona couldn't contain her annoyance any longer. 'My boss. Now if you don't mind, I think you'd better go; I have work to do.' She leaned across the desk to switch her computer on.

He didn't move.

Fiona shifted her gaze from the computer to his face. The tightly pressed lips and the deep furrow of his forehead gave the impression he was annoyed. But it was the intensity of the look he was giving her, which made her skin go cold. She swallowed hard and stood up. Keeping her eyes focused on his face, she pointed to the corridor. 'The lift is that way.'

The flash of anger that flitted across his face made her uneasy, but then he turned abruptly, said a curt goodbye, and walked to the lift.

Fiona watched him until the lift doors had closed, then picked up the telephone and dialled reception. 'Hello Harry, that private investigator is on his way down in the lift… What? You didn't send him up? Well can you make sure he leaves the building? Give me a call if you don't see him go. Thanks.'

Fiona sat down; her gut was churning and she was trembling. There was definitely something about that bloke that was unsettling. She took several deep breaths to calm herself. She had recognised Mark in the photo despite the change in his hair and build. So what did that creep want with him? Then a dreadful thought crossed her mind. Perhaps Mark had lied to Jane. She didn't want to believe it, but maybe he was still married and his wife had hired this PI to get the evidence of his adultery. She needed to tell Jane, but Jane was in Africa and they had agreed no calls unless it was an emergency. Fiona decided that this constituted an emergency.

She picked up her handbag, pulled out a small notepad and lifted up the telephone to dial the new mobile number Jane had given her. Just as she was about to dial, she stopped.

One of the drawers of her desk was slightly open. She never left her desk like that. Her gaze moved to the desktop and the card address system. One of the cards was not in line. She leaned forward and flicked it open at the spot. The card had Jane's name and address on it.

'That bloody private investigator,' she cursed, slowly putting the telephone back on its base. How long had he been hovering around her desk or been in the office? Company policy did not permit anyone to be in the office without a member of staff being present. Reception knew that, but poor Harry hadn't sent him up. This was getting stranger by the minute.

She hugged her handbag, thankful she had taken it with her to the toilet. The thought of him snooping around and touching her things made her feel angry. What else had he been sticking his nose in to?

Fiona slowly looked around and noticed Jane's office door slightly ajar. She left her handbag on the floor under her desk and walked into Jane's office. There was nothing he could have found in here as all the paperwork was locked away in the cupboards. She checked each one was secure before moving to the desk. She opened each of the desk drawers knowing Jane kept nothing in them of any importance and sighed deeply with relief. Nothing had been disturbed. *It's just my imagination,* she thought.

As she was about to leave she noticed Jane's computer was on. Now that was strange for she remembered switching it off last night. She touched the keyboard and a request for a password came up on the monitor. Fiona smiled. He obviously hadn't got very far. She switched off the machine and returned to her own desk.

Her work colleagues were just arriving to start work. She acknowledged their greetings and sat down.

She needed to tell Jane about this but was it safe to call her? She picked up the whole telephone and looked under it, around it and everywhere else. She even tried prising open the mouthpiece, but decided to stop when she saw the strange looks coming from the others in the office.

Gently she replaced the telephone and turned her attention to her computer. Out of the corner of her eye she saw her colleagues return to their work.

They already suspected she was nuts, but now they could believe it. She didn't care. Her main priority was Jane. She would try calling Jane from her home after work. But what if that phone wasn't safe either? Was this paranoia or what? *Pull yourself together girl,* she chastised herself. *Just pick up the phone and call her.* Her hand hovered over the telephone then quickly withdrew.

'What's the matter Fiona, your phone got germs or something?' Sally yelled, from her desk.

Fiona laughed. 'Yeah, it's come out in funny coloured spots.' She heard Sally chuckle as she turned back to her computer. *I'll call her after work, from Jenny's place, just to be sure,* Fiona thought as she pulled her work up on the computer.

That private investigator didn't look like the type to give up easily and that look he gave her. She shivered. What on earth had Jane got herself mixed up in now?

***

Jane and Mark walked out of the security clearance area into the hustle and bustle of Windhoek Khoma airport. She saw a scruffy-looking, slim-built man frantically waving at them and knew it was James when Mark waved back. James looked like he had just come from an archaeological dig, for his linen trousers and shirt were crumpled and pockmarked with ground-in dirt. His long, curly hair fell roughly around his oval, sun-burnt face, but didn't hide the radiant smile he gave them as they reached him.

'Welcome to Namibia, Mark, it's so good to see you.' He shook Mark's hand with such vigour that Jane saw a wave of vibration radiate throughout Mark's body.

'This is Jane,' Mark said, stepping aside.

Jane tentatively held out her right hand and braced herself for the shock wave, but James gently cradled it in both of his and softly pressed his lips to her knuckles.

'It is a great pleasure to meet you, Jane,' he soothed.

Jane felt the rush of a blush hit her face before she had any chance to stop it.

Mark grinned, 'I should have warned you that under this scruffy exterior of his, James is really a gentleman.'

Jane quickly recovered and said, 'It's a pity there aren't more men like him in this world.'

James gently squeezed her hand before releasing it. 'My friends, I am so glad you could come, I really need your help.' He picked up one of their bags and guided them outside.

The heat of the day hit Jane like she was walking into a sauna, causing her to immediately perspire and catch her breath. The dryness of the air prickling her nose and mouth.

'You said something has happened to the crystals in the mine. Have you found out what it is?' Mark asked.

James stopped and looked around cautiously. 'I can't discuss it here. It is better if I show you. We must wait until we get back to my place.'

'Is it that serious?'

James nodded and continued walking. 'And, I think we are only seeing the beginning. Here is my car.'

Jane looked at the battered, rusty old Mercedes and wondered whether it would take the three of them and the luggage without falling apart.

'I see you have come up in the world,' Mark joked as he lifted the baggage into the open boot.

James grinned. 'Well I decided that I needed a new car when the floor under the driving seat of the other one fell out. Luckily I wasn't driving it at the time.'

Jane couldn't hide the worried expression on her face and James picked up on it.

'Oh don't worry my dear, this one is pretty solid, despite its outer looks, and it has air conditioning.' He opened the rear car door for her.

Jane got in and sunk into the soft leather of the seat. The inside was luxurious and had the rich smell of polish. James was quite a character and she was getting to like him very quickly.

Mark sat in the front with James and they drove out of the airport car park.

James informed them that the journey to his place would take nearly an hour, so Jane stared out of the car window, watching the patchy green land gradually give way to barren, rocky dessert.

She let her mind drift back to her earlier conversation with Mark. 'So who is James and how does he know you?' she asked, after Mark mentioned wanting to go to Africa.

'James is a friend who I met about four years ago. He was just finishing a university course on geology.'

'And does he know you as Mark or Adrian?' Jane wanted to make sure she didn't inadvertently cause Mark a problem. Since she discovered that Mark had changed his identity, to avoid a man call Ferrand, she was wary of anyone who said they knew him.

'He knows me as Mark. But he is aware I used to work at NASA, but that's all.'

'So what's in this mine that is so worrying?' she asked.

'Crystals. According to James there is something happening to the crystals.'

'And you're an expert on crystals, are you?' she challenged.

Mark gave a slow, deep shrug. 'I used crystals in my work with NASA and as a engineering scientist I have used them in making precision equipment.'

'What kind of work with NASA or can't you tell me?' she probed expectantly.

'Can't tell you I'm afraid, official secrets and all that.'

Jane remembered feeling frustrated, but she had forced herself to accept his answer.

Her attention returned to the present moment as the car began to slow down.

'Here we are, welcome to my home,' James declared. He turned into the driveway of a large, white, single-storey house, with a red-tiled roof and a veranda along its entire length. It was set well back off the main road and surrounding it was a high, wire fence, with barbed wire angled along the top. Signs, painted with red lightning symbols, were pinned to poles at intervals along the perimeter, warning people not to touch the fence. The closed gates opened when they approached and they drove through to the front of the house.

Jane saw two black African servants, a man and a woman, quickly appeared on the porch. The man was in his mid-thirties, tall and well-built, wearing khaki trousers and a shirt. Hanging from his left shoulder was a rifle. The woman was older, slightly overweight, with short, dark, curly hair. She was wearing a bright patterned dress, partly covered with an apron.

The car stopped and the man stepped forward to open the door for Jane to exit. He then went round to the boot and removed the luggage.

'This is Kwasi, he is my handyman and also looks after my security; and this is Aisha, my house keeper.' James waited until Kwasi had placed the luggage on the porch. He then spoke directly to his servants, 'These are my friends, they are my guests and you will attend to their every need.' Kwasi and Aisha nodded their heads in acknowledgement to James's instructions.

Jane was a little taken back by the abruptness of James's commands and became even more uncomfortable when James prevented her from picking up her bag.

'Kwasi will attend to your luggage. Come inside out of the heat. Aisha, refreshments for my guests.'

Inside, the house was very luxurious and clutter free. Everything had a place and seemed quite out of contrast with James and the visual impression he gave to the outside world.

'Take a seat whilst I change my clothes. Then we'll have some refreshments and I'll explain everything to you.'

Jane sat down on the cotton fabric settee and allowed the cool air of the air conditioning to bathe her exposed skin. Mark moved over to the wall by the door leading to the kitchen, to inspect an African mask and spear displayed there.

Aisha came through the swinging door carrying a tray with a jug of iced lemonade and three glasses. She carefully placed it on the wooden coffee table in front of Jane. Mark called to her before she had a chance to pour the drinks.

'Aisha, are these from around here?'

'Yes boss…' she hesitated as if uncertain she had addressed him correctly.

Mark smiled. 'Just call me, Mark.'

Aisha nodded gratefully and said, 'They are from the Bushmen, the local tribe who walk the land. Master

James spent time with them. The mask is for protection and the spear is for good hunting.'

James reappeared; his hair was brushed back into a ponytail and white cotton slacks and a t-shirt replaced the grubby clothes he had worn. 'Ah, that's better. Come my friends, have a drink. Aisha, that will be all for now.' He waited until she had left before pouring out the drinks. Mark joined Jane on the settee and took the glass offered to him. 'Cheers,' James said, as he took a swig of the lemonade.

Jane let the cool drink linger in her mouth for a few seconds before swallowing. It was beautifully sweet with just a tang of bitterness.

'So James, what's been happening with the crystals?' Mark asked.

James sat down and his face became serious. 'A few weeks ago we began blasting a new section of the mine, where our geological scans had indicated there were large deposits of fluorite to be found.'

He paused and Jane asked, 'Sorry, but what's fluorite?'

James went to a shelf on the wall behind him and brought back a beautiful green crystal point. He gave it to her. 'Fluorite is a calcium fluoride crystal, which comes in various colours. We mainly have green here.'

Jane held it in her left hand. She could feel its vibration and the sensation seemed to create a warm glow in her chest.

James continued, 'Anyway, we began blasting and instead of fluorite we found huge quartz laser wands. I mean really big ones.' James stretched his arms apart to about three feet. 'That was the size of the ones that were dislodged by the blast, but, behind them, further into the rock, were even bigger ones.'

'So you found laser wands, what's the problem?' Mark looked puzzled.

James took another drink of lemonade, then said, 'It's what happened next that has me worried. My men took the loose ones and began cleaning the dirt from them. They didn't notice that inside the quartz points, there were black veins.'

'Another mineral inclusion?' Mark suggested.

'That's what I thought, but the men said it was fluid, so I thought maybe it was discoloured water. I wasn't too bothered about it; the crystals will sell for a better price if there is something unusual within them.'

'So what's got you so worried?'

'We blasted late, so the men only handled three or four of the crystals before leaving for the day. I got a call next morning to say that all three men were off ill and one had been taken to hospital.'

'What happened to them?' Jane asked, putting the fluorite on the table.

'The doctors don't know. The one in hospital is declining fast and they think he could die, but they don't know why. It is like he has given up on life. There are no physical symptoms so they think it's mental, some kind of depression, but they don't understand how it could have affected him so quickly. They are doing tests, but their resources are limited.'

'And the other two?' Mark asked.

'They have similar signs, but they seem better today. I did some checks into their work schedule and it looks like they didn't handle as many of the crystals as Jano, the one in hospital, did. Everyone is refusing to go near the blast site now.'

'Have you had a look at the crystals yourself?' Mark's interest was stirred.

James nodded. 'I looked at the ones they extracted and the black fluid is still inside, but it seems to be getting thicker. Strange, eh? So I didn't touch it.' He fiddled with his glass. 'I then went to the blast wall to look at the larger quartz points. They have the same blackness inside of them and are getting darker every day. This fluid stuff seems to be thickening up at the base before moving up to the point.'

'How can it be the cause of your men's sickness?' Mark was shaking his head.

'I don't know, but I'm taking no chances. I've cordoned off the area for the time being. I'd be grateful if you could have a look with me, tomorrow.'

'Yes of course. Have you done any extractions of the fluid yet?'

'No, I've just quarantined the points in a sealed container and ordered some protective lab suits. They should be here tomorrow,' James paused, 'I'll need help with the analysis. Will you help?'

'Yes, but I think you're being over cautious, there's never been anything bad associated with mining crystals.'

James finished his drink before speaking. 'I know, but if the crystals have been exposed to contaminated water, then my men may have picked up something from the water.' He rubbed his face. 'Mark, this could be bad for me. Namibia takes the protection of its environment very seriously. They could shut me down if they think I have infectious water or land.'

'Let's not jump to any conclusions yet. We'll have a look first.' Mark stifled a yawn, with his hand.

'Oh forgive my manners,' James said, quickly putting his glass down. 'You've had a long journey. I'll get Aisha to show you to your room.' He leapt up, yelling Aisha's name as he moved round the coffee table.

Mark got up and James grasped his hand. 'I'm so glad you came.' James turned to Jane and took the hand she gave him. 'My home is your home, dear lady.'

Aisha came into the room and James gave her instructions before turning back to them saying, 'Rest my friends, dinner will be at eight but if you need anything at all before then, Aisha will get it for you.'

Jane and Mark followed Aisha out of the room, down a narrow corridor to a room at the end. Aisha opened the door and left. The room was large with a huge bed against the wall, opposite the window. A beautifully carved wooden table and matching chairs were to the right of the door, with a wooden wardrobe against the opposite wall. An air-conditioning unit filled the room with cool air and a mosquito screen lined the closed window. A door at the far end, next to the wardrobe, led to a luxuriously tiled bathroom.

Their luggage was stacked on the floor at the base of the bed and Jane noticed something on one of the pillows. She chuckled out loud as she went over to it.

'What?' Mark asked.

Jane picked up the single red rose and realised it was synthetic. 'I think James is a romantic at heart.'

'Hmm,' Mark said, stretching out on top of the bed, 'I think I'm going to have to keep my eye on him.'

★★★

The next morning, Mark and Jane were sitting at the dinning table eating what appeared to be an English breakfast, although Jane wasn't sure that, what she was eating, was bacon. James bustled into the room, dressed in his scruffy clothes again. He quickly sat down and Aisha served him.

'Good morning, did you sleep well?'

Jane smiled, remembering how the bed had swallowed her, cushioning every curve of her body. 'Blissfully,' she said.

'Good, good,' James muttered, as he delved into his breakfast.

'No sore head?' Jane mused, reflecting on the bloodshot eyes and pale colour of his face.

He grinned. 'My dear lady, a bottle or two of our excellent African wine does not produce a hangover.' He held up his hand, as Jane was about to interject. 'But, three or four, in the company of good friends, can produce some adverse effects. Still it was an excellent evening.'

Jane heard a groan from beside her and laughed. Mark had hardly touched his food and was cradling his head in his hands. She nudged him gently. 'You should have stopped when I did.'

He muttered another groan.

'I have a cure for our ailment, Mark. It's an old African remedy. Disgusting to taste, but works a treat.' James indicated to Aisha and she left the room returning a few minutes later with two glasses containing some dark, mucky-brown fluid.

Jane was glad she wasn't drinking it.

An hour later, Jane and Mark got into James's car and they set off for the mine. James's miracle cure for the hangover had worked and Mark was beginning to look more like himself. His tanned face had lost the pale flashes and the sparkle in his brown eyes had returned.

Jane was curious about the mine. 'Do we have to go down deep to see these crystals?'

James chuckled. 'No, no. The mine is an open cast one. We blast away the rock surface to expose the veins or pockets of crystals held in the earth.'

'Isn't that destructive? I mean you're creating a hole in the ground.'

'Yes, but least you can see it. When mining underground, there could be many layers of tunnels crossing under where you are walking or driving and you won't know they are there, until the ground gives in.'

Jane didn't like the thought of that nor did she like the thought of mining above ground. She prepared herself for what she was about to see, as they approached the mine's gates.

The single security guard recognised James and opened the gates as the car approached. James drove straight through. The land, past the entrance, was rocky and barren. A track road split into two, a little way ahead, with the right one swinging down to a huge crater, where men were working at the rock face. They were pulling out crystal structures and placing them in barrels. The left track took them round a rock cliff to a smaller quarry, where more men were working. James drove past them, following the road round and down until they reached a barrier preventing any further travel. It was a temporary one, made of large metal drums, spread across the road with a large sign painted in red, saying, "DANGER – ENTRY PROHIBITED".

Jane felt a nervous twinge in her stomach, as the three of them left the car and walked between the drums.

The track continued a little way up before dropping to a small area against the cliff face. A few outbuildings stood a short distance away to the left and they walked towards them. Just before they got to the buildings, James moved to the right, into what seemed to be a small alcove in the rock. Jane followed him; the anxiousness in her body was building.

James stopped about five feet from the rock wall and Mark moved to stand beside him. Jane heard James gasp, and when she drew level with him, he said, 'It's almost totally black now. This is not normal, Mark.'

There exposed, in about a ten-foot area, she saw a large black crystal. Mark moved forward slightly and James quickly pulled him back. 'No closer, I don't know how safe we are without protective suits.'

It was at that moment that Jane felt a huge heaviness fall across her shoulders. It was like someone had shrouded her in a heavy coat, which pressed hard against her neck. She dropped her head forward and her nose became stuffed up, so much so, she had to open her mouth to breathe. Feelings of sadness, misery and despair suddenly overwhelmed her, and she began to cry.

James and Mark immediately turned to look at her, shock and puzzlement on their faces.

Quickly, James scooped her into his arms and swiftly

carried her away from the rock face to the buildings. Mark rushed ahead, opening the door. Inside, James gently lowered her onto a chair and Mark pulled up a chair to sit beside her.

Jane wiped away her tears with a tissue James gave her. She had no idea what had caused her distress. The heaviness was now gone and so too, the stuffiness in her head. Gradually a feeling of warmth was filling her, just as if she was sat by an open fire. She smiled at the two anxious faces staring at her. 'I'm fine now, really, I'm okay.'

'What happened?' Mark asked, his hand taking hold of hers.

'I don't know. It came on really quickly. A heavy, depressed feeling with so much misery and despair. I've never felt anything like it before. But it's gone now, thank goodness.'

James stood up and paced the room. 'It's the same as what my men described, but you didn't touch it. Dear God, that means, whatever it is, has gone airborne.'

'Just hang on a minute, James, if that was the case, you and I would have felt it.'

James stopped pacing, the index finger, of this right hand tapping his chin. 'Perhaps Jane is more sensitive than we are.'

Mark stood up. 'But it wouldn't explain why she feels better now. If it was a viral gone airborne, she would still be unwell, but she isn't.'

'Good point, good point. Still I'm going to see if our lab suits have come before we do anything else.' James left the room.

Jane noticed Mark frowning.

'What's up?'

'I was thinking about what just happened, it makes no sense, unless...'

'What?'

'How did you feel as you approached the rock face?'

'I was anxious.'

'Anything else?' Mark was really focused on her.

'I don't think so. Not until we stopped and then it was like I had impacted on something, which fell over me.'

Mark's face had gone pale. 'It's not possible, surely.'

'What's not possible?'

Just then James returned carrying a box. Mark squeezed Jane's arm. 'I'll tell you what I think it is once I've done some tests, then I'll know for sure.'

Jane nodded, knowing she would get nothing more from him.

James placed the box on the desk and opened it. 'We should be ok with these,' he said, unpacking what looked like a space-suit.

Mark felt the texture and shook his head. 'We can't go near the rock face with these.'

James looked disappointed. 'But they're from my friend who works in the UK's infectious diseases centre and they deal with some lethal bugs.'

'It's not infectious diseases we need protection from, it's the vibration from the crystals.'

'What do you mean?' Jane asked, seeing the puzzlement on James's face too.

Mark looked at them for a moment, then said, 'Our

bodies are surrounded by a ball of energy, which feeds our body; you may know it as the aura. All sorts of things can impact on it and I think that what you experienced, is the crystal's vibration impacting on your energy system.'

Jane recalled how she had felt and nodded. 'Yes, that's exactly how it was. One minute I was okay, the next I felt horrible.' She shivered slightly.

Mark took her hand and squeezed it. 'Crystals vibrate at different levels and quartz crystals are very strong in their vibration. You must be sensitive to it.' He paused like he had thought of something.

'What is it?' Jane asked.

'You said you felt horrible. The crystals must be sending out negative vibrations.'

James looked at the suit in his hands. 'And vibrations travel through anything. So how are we going to do this?'

'We need to, somehow, get a sample of the black stuff without us going near the crystal.'

James smiled. 'I have exactly the thing and I've been dying to use it. I'm going to get, Roger.' He promptly left the room.

Jane looked at Mark and he just shrugged his shoulders. 'I told you he was eccentric.'

CHAPTER TWO

It took James nearly two hours to set up "ROGER", the "Remotely Operated Gatherer of Earth Rocks", so that its robotic arms could use a drill. ROGER was used to enter small, and often unstable, tunnels to obtain samples of crystals. It was only three feet tall, with caterpillar legs, and crab-like claws, at the end of two moveable arms.

He finally stood up, looking very pleased with himself.

Mark bent down to fit a bit into the drill end. 'This diamond bit should do the work.'

'Why a diamond one?' Jane asked, trying to see the diamond.

'Quartz has a hardness that will dull normal metal drill bits, even ones that have cobalt titanium coatings. Only a diamond bit has a hardness greater than quartz and so will cut through it.' He secured the bit and stood up.

'But why do you need the water?' She pointed to the water-pipe spray end strapped to the other arm of the robot.

James answered her. 'My dear, when you drill anything, you create friction and this causes heat to build up, which can break the crystal. And, we wouldn't want anything to get out.'

Jane frowned at him. 'But you're creating a hole anyway, so what is inside *is* going to get out.'

James took her hand and gently patted it. 'Don't you worry, we have created a crystal plug.' He pointed to the tiny crystal point being held in the jaws of the robot's claw.

'James, let's do this,' Mark called, as he began pulling on the lab suit.

James turned away from Jane and joined Mark at the desk.

'But you said, these suits can't stop the vibrations; that ROGER was going to the rock face,' Jane said anxiously, her stomach tightening.

Mark was at her side in minutes, he gently took her in his arms. 'Don't worry,' he said softly. 'We're not going to the face. ROGER will drill for the dark stuff and bring the drill bit back with a sample on it. Once the dark stuff is free from the crystal we'll need to examine it, hence the suits. We'll do this in the lab, at the end of the building. It has a phone, so I'll call you once it's done.'

He kissed her on the lips and Jane held him tightly. No matter how hard she tried to calm her mind, her thoughts always focused on something going wrong and this could be the last time she would ever hold him.

He tried to pull away, but she held on to him, not wanting this moment to be over. She finally eased away. 'You be careful,' she whispered.

He nodded and, picking up his gloves and head protection, made for the door.

James picked up the remote controller and when he passed her, he said, 'He's in safe hands, my dear, I promise.'

Jane nodded, registering the dread filling her stomach. She hated saying goodbye and being left behind. The last time it had happened to her, she had lost her parents.

Now her mind was reliving the guilt she felt, in letting her parents go without her. She watched Mark, ROGER and James leave the room, resisting the urge to run after them.

***

Mark entered the lab, setting his gloves down on the table in the centre of the room. The lab was small, but fully equipped. Two microscopes stood three feet away from each other, on a worktop, at the far end of the room. A sink and cleansing materials took up part of another wall and a large refrigerator stood against the wall, where the door was. A window, situated between two other worktops, completed the final wall, which faced the rock face.

Mark went straight to the window and watched James outside, manoeuvring ROGER into position, a direct line to the crystal. His stomach churned with worry. If his assumptions were proved correct, it meant someone had got hold of his research and implemented the very thing that had caused him to stop. He shivered. He didn't want to believe it; he hoped with every beat of his heart, he was wrong. He glanced across to the other building, glimpsing Jane's concerned face in the window. Somehow Jane knew. Her ability to sense things had developed since their time with Jasmine.

"You must tell her soon, brother." Angie's voice came into his mind. He felt a warmth fill his heart, as he remembered his last conversation with his sister. 'I will,' he whispered.

The flash of James' body moving, across his view, to the lab door, brought his thoughts back to what they were doing. He turned his attention to ROGER.

James came through the door and joined him at the window. 'All set to go,' he announced, then flicked the lever of the remote control forward and ROGER began its trip to the crystal. It took ten minutes to reach the rock face, as James was unfamiliar with the controller.

Mark watched through binoculars. 'Stop!' he commanded.

James took his hand from the controls, then pulled down his hands-free binoculars to cover his eyes.

'Let's go slowly forward until the bit is touching the crystal,' Mark instructed.

'With you on that one,' James said, as he tried to ease the tiny control stick gently away from him.

ROGER suddenly jumped forward, hitting the crystal hard. 'Ops! Sorry about that; this controller is really sensitive.'

'Perhaps we should have let Jane do this,' Mark muttered.

James turned to him, pushing the binoculars up on to his forehead. 'Let a beautiful lady do this dangerous task? Mark, I'm surprised at you for even suggesting it.'

Mark smiled. 'You're showing your up-bringing now.'

James snorted and returned his attention to what he was doing.

Mark knew James came from a very wealthy family, but had for years, been trying to live his life away from the pomp and prudishness of the aristocracy, especially his mother. But, every so often, it slipped out, more so when a woman was around.

'ROGER is in place and the drill is ready,' James said, putting down the remote and exiting the door. A few seconds later, he was back. 'Water is on.' He retrieved the remote and pressed a button. 'Drilling has started,' he declared.

Through the binoculars, Mark could see ROGER drilling at the crystal edge, where the darkness was only about an inch from the surface. Within five minutes, the drill had hit the blackness, and he thought he could see it swirling, which meant the blackness was fluid. He hoped it was just water.

James stopped the drill and retracted the bit. As soon as it was clear, he raised the other claw and pushed the crystal plug into the hole. It fit snugly. He immediately put the remote down and went outside to switch off the water. When he returned, he began guiding ROGER back towards them.

Mark went to the table to put his head and glove protection on. After a final check that everything was sealed, he went outside and waited for James to bring ROGER up to him. The robot stopped and Mark retrieved the drill bit into a sterile test-tube glass container. He noticed the bit was covered in tiny, black crystal particles. He sealed the container and returned to the lab.

James was ready in his own suit when Mark entered. 'It doesn't look like contaminated water,' Mark said, hardly able to hide his disappointment. He placed the container, in a holder, next to the microscope. 'It seems to be crystalline.'

James looked at the bit closely. 'But how can that be?

'I don't know,' Mark lied.

'Well, let's get started and see what we can find,' James said, rubbing his hands together.

Mark wasn't so enthusiastic. He knew that, if the tests proved it was what he thought it was, he would have some explaining to do.

* * *

Hours passed and the waiting was becoming unbearable. Jane paced the room, willing the phone to ring when suddenly it did. She rushed over to it and snatched it off the docking station. 'Hello?' she blustered.

'Are you okay?' It was Mark.

'Yes. Yes, of course. What news?'

'We've done some tests, but it's late and we're going to leave it till tomorrow. Be with you in a few minutes.'

She put down the phone and quickly moved to the window. After five minutes, she saw them coming towards her in their ordinary clothes. When they came through the door, they both looked tired and worried.

'What is it?' she asked immediately.

Mark sat down and gave a big sigh. 'It looks like the crystal structure is changing.'

'What does that mean?' Jane asked confused. She began to feel anxious, when Mark didn't answer her. She turned to James.

'Crystals are made up of atoms and these atoms form a ordered structure, which repeats itself. The smallest repeating pattern is called a unit cell and it has the same symmetry as the entire crystal. When these units are three dimensionally packed, they form a crystal lattice.'

'James…' Jane shook her head, 'In a language I can understand, please,' she pleaded.

James smiled. 'The crystal is the same right down to its smallest part, its atoms. The atoms are like balls, or molecules, that are joined together in a certain pattern, and this pattern makes up the structure.'

'So it's changing, what's wrong with that?'

'Some how, this black crystallised fluid has got into the crystal and changed the balance and structure of the atoms.' James answered.

'And that's bad?' Jane asked, still not understanding.

'Disastrous,' Mark said, suddenly.

Jane turned to him. 'Why, what will it do?'

Mark seemed to ignore her question as he went on, 'We froze the water around the crystallised particles and then examined it. The crystal structure of the water, is awful. Do you remember, at Jasmine's, when she showed us photos of frozen water exposed to negative words or music?'

'Yes, the crystal shapes were like bubbling black oil. Is that what the water looks like?' Jane licked her lips as her mouth started to go dry.

Mark nodded. 'It looks like the atoms of the crystal have been exposed to some kind of negative…' he paused as if trying to find the right word. '…virus or fluid, and it's affecting everything it comes into contact with, including us.'

There was silence.

'We need to tell someone, the authorities, maybe,' Jane stammered.

'Now, let's not be too hasty,' James said quickly. ' We don't know for sure this is happening.'

'But your tests, your men in hospital,' Jane countered.

'Tests are not conclusive yet and we need to get some tests done on James' men, before we go raising alarms,' Mark said.

'I don't understand you two. You said, this could be serious.'

'We want to be sure about this, before we do anything. We need another day.' Mark gently put his arm around her and Jane relaxed into him, only now realising how stressed she had become. She sighed and said, 'I'm just worried, that's all.'

'My dear lady, you're worried? I have forty men working here and the possibility that I'll have to close the mine and lay them all off, but am I worried? Hell yes, so until I'm sure I've something to be really concerned about, I'm just going to take pre-cautions.' James moved over to the door and looked back at them. 'It'll take about half an hour.' Then he was gone.

Jane turned to Mark, she could see the strain on his face turn to a worried frown. 'What is it?' she asked frustrated.

'Nothing.'

'It's not nothing!' she said forcefully. 'I've seen that look before, it was when you thought I had responded to that Internet "Missing Poster" of you.'

Mark looked at her. 'I just want one more day of tests and then I'll be sure.'

'Sure about what?'

'That it's what I think it is.'

Jane looked at him puzzled, then a moment of realisation hit her. 'You've seen this before, haven't you?'

Mark turned away, hiding his face from her. 'Maybe.'

Jane took his arm and turned him back to her, so she could see his expression. 'Maybe! You either have or not, the truth, Mark.'

Pain flashed across his face, as he appeared to remember something. 'It may have come from some research I was doing.'

Jane couldn't believe she was hearing his words. 'You! You caused this?'

'Yes, and No! I didn't do this, I swear. Somehow, someone has either, got hold of my research or, they came to this result with something they have been doing themselves, I don't know.'

'So what is it?'

'Please, Jane, I need one more day and then I'll tell you everything. I promise.'

Jane saw the stooped, despondent appearance of his body and when she looked into his eyes, her heart seemed to melt, for there was such sadness. 'You promise?' she said firmly.

Mark just nodded his head without responding.

She took hold of his hand and squeezed it. 'Then, that's good enough for me.' She saw his head turn towards her and a relieved smile touch his lips.

'Thank you,' he whispered.

The door opened and James came bustling through, struggling with a large, well-grown, potted tree. 'You said, you wanted a plant. It's a Quiver tree. Will this do?' He dumped it firmly on the floor in front of them. When he stood straight, a puzzled expression appeared on his face. ' Did I miss something?'

Jane smiled. 'Not yet. Tomorrow, James. We'll all know, tomorrow.'

'Right. Good. So let's go home and open a bottle, I need a drink.'

'Just one thing to do, before we go,' Mark said, picking up the potted tree and going outside with it.

Jane and James followed him, stopping by the door. They watched Mark carry the pot and tree, to about ten feet from the crystal rock face, and place it on the ground.

'What's he doing?' James asked.

'Beats me, but tomorrow we may have our answers.'

CHAPTER THREE

The next day, they returned to the mine. It was silent and empty, for James had given the men the day off. As they walked from the car, Jane could feel Mark's anxiousness through the grip he had on her hand, and when they were in sight of the plant, she felt Mark's body stiffen.

'What on earth?' James muttered, quickening his pace towards it.

'STAY AWAY FROM IT!' Mark yelled, jumping forward and grabbing his arm.

James stopped abruptly. 'What the hell is going on?'

Jane stared at what had been a beautiful, lush Quiver tree. All that was left of its green, Aloe Vera-type leaves were withered black tentacles, knurled into twisted bone-like fingers. Its light trunk had blackened and split, spilling its shrivelled insides in lava-like flows down its peeling dead layers of bark. It had died a terrible death.

Mark let go of James's arm and sat down on a slab of rock. 'I didn't want this to happen.'

'It's time you told us what you know,' James said, turning towards him.

Mark nodded and took a deep breath. Jane placed her hand on his shoulder and when he looked up, she said, 'It's okay.' She saw a flash of fear touch his eyes and she began to worry. What if, what he was going to say, wasn't going to be okay?

Mark looked away and began to speak, 'It started

many years ago, when I lived in America, with my ex-wife. I was doing some private research at home…'

★★★

Mark remembered working with the crystals. They were natural stones, but with a life force all of their own. They each felt different every time he held one, and it was their vibration and their use in electronics that intrigued him. He knew their structure made it possible for them to create electricity and that quartz crystals were the ones that produced the purest output. He wanted to see if he could create a more efficient energy source for the world, by enhancing the vibration of crystals to produce more energy.

He knew that a pure crystal, one without any blemishes or inclusions, was very rare in nature, but was the best one to program. Luckily, with modern science, this crystal could be man-made by using a seed crystal. Nearly every electrical unit contained this type of crystal.

Mark's thoughts returned to the day it all began…

He struggled into the kitchen, his arms laden with lab equipment. Carefully, he placed them on the kitchen table and heard an exasperated cry.

'Damn it! What do you think you're doing?'

Mark turned quickly, only now seeing his wife, Solita, at the back door. 'I'm going to do some research at home.' He saw the look of shock on her face.

'You can't.'

Mark frowned. 'Why?'

Solita seemed to struggle finding the words, then said, 'Cause there's no room.'

'I'm going to use the basement. You don't use it, so I won't be in your way.'

'But, you can't work here, every day. I… I have the children to care for.'

Mark chuckled. 'I'm not going to be working here, all day, I still have my job to do.' He opened the basement door and switched on the light, before picking up his equipment. 'This is something I want to do for myself.'

He descended the stairs and placed the equipment onto a wooden table in the centre of the room.

Solita called down to him, 'So this will be done, in your own time, will it?'

'Yes,' he yelled back.

'Good.'

The almost joyous tone of her voice made Mark turn to look back up the stairs, but Solita had gone.

The next few days, after work, were busy with setting up the lab and bringing in the materials he needed to carry out the experiments. Surprisingly, Solita didn't complain or moan about the time he was taking, in fact, she was very encouraging.

The weekend came and on Saturday morning, Solita offered to take the children out, so he could do more work. She had hardly left the house, when Mark was down in the basement. He couldn't contain his excitement, for he had created a ten-inch pure crystal point earlier in the week and his experiments from this had resulted in a crystallised fluid, which he had introduced to the crystal point to enhance it.

He had since examined the crystal, using highly specialised equipment in his lab at work and what he discovered had surprised him. The crystal was shining from the inside. Somehow the crystallised fluid had entered the matrix of the crystal structure itself. It had filled the spaces between the crystal's atoms and created a new lattice structure.

As Mark walked down the stairs, he saw the crystal point on the table. It was held on a plastic support, shaped like metal prongs used to hold a skewer for spit roasts. The crystal was glowing in the light from the fluorescent light above it.

Today, he was going to see how the change to its make up would affect its vibration. He placed electric connections to the crystal and sent electricity into it at a low rate. Amazingly, the crystal began to glow brighter, shining like a star, glistening like a diamond. He could feel its vibration from a foot away and it was getting stronger.

For hours, he watched and noted the change in the crystal's vibration and brightness. It didn't seem to diminish or change and the readings of its output were strong and steady, even with the low power input.

He heard the front door and Solita coming in. He disconnected the electric from the crystal and placed a potted plant close to it. *I wonder how the crystal energy will enhance this plant?* he thought to himself. Finally, he recorded the time and the current strength of the crystal's vibration and scribbled a note against it: "Check if any energy is left in crystal, in the morning."

He climbed the stairs, back up to the kitchen, feeling happy and full of energy. Solita was at the kitchen sink and he quickly wrapped his arms around her waist. She wriggled out of his hold and pushed him away.

'What's up with you?' she said, annoyed.

Mark smiled. 'Nothing, I feel good that's all and I wanted to hold you.'

'I'm busy making dinner.' She stared at him and her eyes scrutinised his face. 'You've been drinking.'

'I have not. I've only just come up. Didn't even have time for lunch or a break.' Her accusation didn't seem to dent his happy feeling and he said, 'I'll go play with the children, then.'

Mark hadn't reached the door before Solita was blocking his way.

She smiled sweetly. 'As you have SO much energy, you can make dinner. I am whacked out.' She kissed him on the lips and before he could wrap his arms around her, she had slipped away.

***

On Sunday, Solita had dressed the children and was on her way out of the front door before Mark had even finished his breakfast. He had slept the best sleep he could ever remember and felt wonderful.

Down in the basement, Mark discovered that the crystal was still glowing brightly, despite receiving no further energy from the electric connections. Even the plant seemed to be giving off a healthy glow and its leaves were the brightest green he had ever seen. His stomach buzzed with exhilaration. Could this be the start of self-perpetuating energy?

He wondered if he could program the crystal to vibrate even more. Could he use another energy source, a natural one? In his mind, a memory came of his time travelling, when he was young. He remembered learning from the indigenous people, in South America, of a way of bringing down universal energy.

This was a powerful energy that the Shamans said could not be controlled. The process had to be done with respect and with no intended outcome. It was rarely carried out, for the effect of the power could not be predicted and there was no way of knowing what it would do. It could enhance or destroy.

Mark looked at the crystal he had made. With universal power, the crystal could produce sustainable energy and it wouldn't cost anything once the system was set up. There would be unlimited energy for everyone.

He sat for a moment looking at the crystal and plant. His enthusiasm was bursting to move ahead but could he remember the technique they used? Did he have the skills they had? Slowly he began to recall what he needed to do and although he knew he didn't have their medicine bundles or other sacred objects, he was sure that he could control the energy with his new crystal.

Taking the crystal from its holder, he laid it on a white cloth on the floor and knelt over it. He called in the elements of Earth, Water, Air and Fire, then began to chant in the sacred language of the tribe that had taught him. Calling to Father Sun to bless him with the power of the universe, he raised his arms to the sky reaching for the energy. He felt it tapping on his fingers and when he opened his hands, it whooshed down through him into the crystal.

He sat back, his whole body tingling and vibrating. For a moment he thought the energy was stuck within him but the feelings began to fade and he was left with a spaced-out wooziness in his head. He picked up the crystal, watching how intensely it was glowing, the energy inside expanding outwards until the crystal was surrounded in an amazing white light. The light grew denser until it manifested into a small ball of energy, nestling in his hands. The vibration of the crystal caused the ball to grow bigger and bigger, turning it into a mass of swirling energy, which Mark struggled to control. He placed it on the floor and watched the energy ball grow even bigger, spreading outwards. It completely enveloped the cloth and Mark realised it was out of control. If he didn't do something soon, it would engulf the whole room.

Quickly he placed his homemade insulator-conductor unit over the top of the ball and began siphoning off the energy into two large batteries. Gradually the ball disappeared and the batteries became full. Mark removed the unit and picked up the crystal, it was shinning even brighter now and he wondered how much of the energy was still in the crystal. He placed it back on its holder and took the batteries outside. Despite the small hiccup he had controlling the power, he was pleased with the result.

Solita came home, as he was writing his notes.

'Busy day?' she said pleasantly.

He put his pen down. 'I think I have found a way to produce free and safe energy.'

'Free energy? That's not going to make any money.' She sounded disappointed. 'Can't we produce and sell it?'

Mark laughed. 'No. That's not what I've done it for. Just think of a world where energy is abundant and we are not ripping great holes in the earth, by mining or risking meltdown from nuclear plants. Our children will grow up in a cleaner, safer environment.'

Solita glanced at his notes. 'Keeping a record of what you've done?'

'Yes, but I need to do more tests.'

'Who are you going to contact about this?'

Mark closed his notebook. 'Let's not rush this. I need to recreate the experiment and make sure the results are the same.'

'We could sell your research,' Solita suggested.

'No. Haven't you heard what I said?' Mark got up frustrated.

Solita quickly moved over to him. 'Don't be angry,' she said, gently taking his face in her hands. 'I just want a secure future for the children.'

Mark relaxed into her body. 'They have a secure future, my job pays for all we need.'

'But what if something should happen to you?'

Mark pulled away and looked at her. 'You're not planning to kill me off, are you?' he said, jokingly.

'No!' Solita looked shocked, then her face softened. 'I meant, if you left us or lost your job.'

Mark squeezed her arms and said, 'No chance about any of that happening, so don't worry.' He caught a glimpse of what seemed annoyance on her face, but she smiled and said, 'Want to help with dinner?'

★★★

The next day Mark got up late and didn't have time to check his work in the basement before he had to go to work. During the morning he received a call.

'Mr Stevenson, my name is Lucan Ferrand. I believe you are doing some interesting work with energy? I'd like to meet with you.'

Mark was shocked, he had told no one about his research, except Solita. 'And who may you be?'

'Let's say I'm a fellow scientist and owner of a private enterprise working on energy solutions. Our meeting could be advantageous to you.'

'Thanks Mr Ferrand, but I am not ready to discuss my work with anyone at the moment.'

There was silence, then Ferrand said, 'I'll call you back tomorrow when you've had time to think. You'd be wise to meet me.'

The undertone of a threat in his last words annoyed Mark. 'Goodbye, Mr Ferrand.'

When Mark returned home at the end of the day, Solita was out, which was just as well for he was still annoyed that knowledge of his research had got to this man, Ferrand. It could have only come from her. He went directly to the basement and was amazed to find that it was filled with brightness despite no light being on. As he descended the stairs, he could see the crystal was awash with light, radiating out into the room and its vibration could be felt from the top of the stairs. All traces of the mood he was in vanished and immense pleasure and contentment replaced it.

On reaching the table he observed that the plant had grown bigger and was stunningly beautiful. The crystal appeared to be generating more and more energy, with the vibration spreading to everything in the room. Even the moss, on the small, dusty window on the far wall, was growing thicker and richer in colour as it absorbed the crystal's energy. He viewed parts of the plant and found its leaves were smooth and soft to touch. Under the microscope, its cellular structure was alive with light. Mark thought his heart would burst with the happiness he felt.

He heard a noise behind him and turned to see Solita at the bottom of the cellar stairs. She was staring at the crystal and plant with wide eyes.

Mark was excited to see her. 'See what's happening? Isn't it great?'

She moved over to the table almost in a trance. Her face seemed to lighten and fill with reverence, a look Mark had never seen on her before. He moved closer and put his arms around her, the love in him for her was overwhelming.

Solita looked into his eyes and for a moment there was a connection of unconditional love, a moment of peace, but as Mark touched his lips to hers, she closed her eyes and pulled back.

'Why do you do that?' he moaned.

'Do what?' she snapped.

'Stop me from getting close to you,' he said softly.

'You're imagining it. Anyway you pick the most inappropriate moments.'

Mark looked at the crystal with a hint of sadness.

Solita shook her body, as if shaking off something and said, 'I got a call today from Mr Ferrand. Why didn't you agree to meet him?'

The memory of the phone conversation brought back Mark's annoyance. 'I'm not going to discuss my research with just anybody. How the hell did he find out about it? Was it you?'

'Yes. He's a friend and he's prepared to offer us a substantial sum of money to have your research.'

Mark became angry. 'How dare you do this behind my back. My research is not for sale.'

'You're being selfish. The money could set us up for life!'

'I don't care, I'm not selling it and that's final.' Mark heaved in a breath and, deciding it was the end of the matter, he turned away from her.

Solita grabbed his left arm, sinking her long nails into his flesh. 'This isn't finished.'

Mark whirled round, yanking his arm out of her grip, causing her nails to gouge deep ruts into his skin, making it bleed. 'You bitch!' he yelled, staring at the trickle of blood slipping down his arm. 'What's got into you?' He grabbed a cloth and held it to the wound. 'I'm not discussing this any further.'

Solita swung round to the table and grabbed the crystal point. She gripped it tightly and pointed it at Mark. 'You had better reconsider selling your research; otherwise I'll destroy everything you've ever worked for. Your pathetic life won't be worth living by the time I'm finished with you.'

Mark felt the force of her venomous rage hit him like a ball of fire; it seared into his skin and created pain in every nerve of his face. He snatched the crystal off her. 'Get out of here! GET OUT!'

Solita stepped back. 'This isn't over, do you hear?' She turned abruptly and stamped her way back up the stairs.

Mark replaced the crystal on its holder, his heart beating wildly. He had never experienced such hatred from Solita and it upset him. He slumped heavily into his chair and thought long and hard about what had just happened. He knew their relationship hadn't always been good, but this was new and it worried him. A few feet from him was the wine rack and a bottle of Merlot caught his eye. Within an hour he had drunk two bottles.

Feeling rather fuzzy and unsteady on his feet, he staggered to the stairs, where he paused for a moment to check where his feet should go. On glancing back, he noticed that the crystal had dulled a bit, but he was too drunk to even want to register this in his notes. Step by step he moved up the stairs until he was in the kitchen.

Solita was sat at the table, a tissue in her hand. 'I'm sorry for what I said. I didn't mean it. I only want what's best for the children.'

Mark put a drunken arm around her shoulders, 'I'm sssorry toooo.' He kissed her hard on the head.

Solita got up and put her arm around him, supporting his body. 'Let's get you to bed, ' she said quietly.

* * *

Mark woke the next morning with a headache determined to punch its way out of his skull. He felt completely drained and hardly able to get out of bed. He carefully walked to the bathroom, shielding his eyes from the sun streaming through the window. After a shower and two Paracetamol he made his way downstairs to the kitchen. The house was quiet, which meant that Solita and the children must have gone out. After some toast and a strong cup of coffee, he almost felt normal again.

He went down to the basement and the first thing he noticed was the light in the room was dull, sombre almost. He switched on the overhead light and immediately saw that the plant next to the crystal had turned black, its leaves all shrivelled up as if it had died in agony. His attention turned to the crystal; it had turned a filthy brown colour with a centre black strip running through it, to its tip. An overwhelming feeling of sadness filled him and he slumped down into the chair next to the table. How could this have happened? What made his beautiful, bright crystal change so quickly? Then he remembered the argument with Solita and how she had held the crystal while shouting at him. He realised that, somehow, Solita had re-programmed the crystal and the consequence was its vibration had killed the plant.

Mark didn't want to believe it. It had been a silly row, but its effect through the crystal had been devastating. This crystal had been created to generate pure, healthy energy, but in the wrong hands it could generate negativity. His thoughts turned to the increase effect of using universal energy on a crystal programmed with negative energy and his skin went cold. If one little crystal could destroy a plant, what would a large one be capable of?

The batteries he had put outside flashed through his mind and taking the steps two at a time, he went out to where he had left them. What he saw caused his legs to go weak and he had to steady himself against the side of the house. The batteries had melted, and a circle of land around them, spreading out two hundred yards, had been destroyed. Every blade of grass, plant and flower had died and turned black.

Mark heard the medicine man's words in his head. *'You cannot control the outcome of the energy you bring down. It will either enhance or bring life, or it will destroy it. It must be respected and tended. If you do not care for it, it will take what it needs.'*

He hadn't done any of that; he had been so sure he could control it, he hadn't considered the consequences of it getting out of control. His stubbornness and arrogance had created this.

Mark returned to the basement feeling depressed. What had started out as a good idea had just developed into the worst thing he had ever done. The crystal on the table had changed again; the blackness inside had spread so that it covered two thirds of its interior. The more he looked at it, the more miserable he became. *What was causing that blackness?* he wondered, and reached out to pick up the crystal. Before his hand touched it, he stopped. The crumbling, dead plant caught his eye and he moved back, searching for some gloves to put on. He found some and returned to the crystal with his vibration testing equipment and a small drill. Surprisingly the crystal's vibration was still emanating from its point at quite a high level, but lower than it had been. He left the connectors on and drilled a small hole so that the drill bit touched the blackness. It was fluid like oil, which seemed to stick to the bit end. Under the microscope he noticed that it was growing and changing the crystalline structure. It was something he had never seen before and he became anxious.

Mark continued to experiment, he took a sample from the plant and examined it under another microscope; its cells had been completely obliterated. He then took a small sample of his own blood and checked the structure of the cells, they looked normal but after he had exposed the slide to the crystal for an hour, he noticed that the cells had started to deteriorate.

The crystal's vibration was affecting anything it came in contact with, including him. He slipped off the chair and moved over to the stairs where he sat down heavily. He felt exhausted and so tired that he just wanted to sleep. His head felt too heavy for his neck and so he let it drop to rest on his knees. His mind didn't want to continue, what was the point anymore?

He didn't know how long he stayed there, but it was Solita's voice calling down to him that brought him back to reality.

'Adrian. Adrian!'

'What is it?' Mark groaned, looking up.

'It's a call for you.'

'Who… is… it?' The words struggled to escape his lips.

'Mr Ferrand. He wants a word.'

Mark dropped his head back on to his knees.

'Well are you going to speak to him?'

Mark didn't respond.

'Adrian? ADRIAN ANSWER ME!' she screeched.

'NO!' Mark shouted back. He heard Solita snort in frustration and slam the basement door.

Mark glared back up the stairs and got to his feet; his hands turning into fists. He wanted to rush up there and… and… TEAR THE BITCH APART! Grip her throat so hard and tight that her skin would split and rip. Then he would stuff her mouth with her own voice box. The rawness and savageness of his thoughts were exploding inside of him. He backed away until the edge of the table brought him to a stop. Swinging round, he hammered the table, until the pain in his hands made him stop. The fierce emotions eased away with the pain and when he looked at the bleeding cuts to his knuckles, tears came to his eyes. What had gotten into him?

He wiped the blood away and glanced over to the crystal, which was now completely black. The vibration detector had also dropped to zero. Curious, Mark connected some electric probes to the crystal and sent electricity into it. The vibration detector still remained at zero. It looked like the crystal had been consumed by the black fluid and no longer could vibrate. He stared at it and thought heavily about what had just happened and it concerned him. This was not what he wanted.

Quickly he picked up his notebooks, the crystal, the plant, his experimental slides and carried them up stairs. When he entered the kitchen, Solita was at the kitchen table, she stood abruptly ready to confront him.

'Don't say anything!' he commanded, pushing his hand out towards her in a stopping action, before moving past and out the back door.

Outside he dumped all his research in a metal barrel in

the middle of the devastated garden and set fire to it. He watched the fire consume the words on the paper, spark brightly as it whooshed through the plant and flicker fiercely as it melted the glass slides. The crystal, he placed in a cloth, on a stone, and smashed it with a sledgehammer. Scraping all its bits together and wrapping the cloth up round them, he threw it all into the fire. The flames shot upwards in a raging plume of fierce heat, before slowly dying back down.

Mark stared into the last flickering flames with remorse. He should have listened to the wisdom of the Elders. Understood their teachings and respected what they had imparted to him. Luckily no real harm had been done, but it could have been worse. He lifted his head and looked up towards the blue sky and brilliant sun. The warm rays seemed to feed his body and lift his mood, soon making him feel more like his normal self. He didn't know what it was he had created in the crystal, but it had a terrible effect on everything and he was glad it was gone.

He returned to the kitchen and found Solita standing at the top of the stairs to the basement. He thought she was smiling, but when she saw him her expression immediately changed to anger.

'What do you think you're doing?'

'I've destroyed my work.'

'Destroyed? Why?'

'Because I wanted to.'

Solita strode across the room and shoved him in the chest. 'You! It's always you, isn't it. What about us? You've thrown away our chance to be rich.'

Mark pushed past her, keeping his emotions in check. 'I told you my research wasn't for sale.'

He reached the basement door and heard her shout, 'You're going regret this!'

Mark ignored her and went down the stairs to clear up his equipment.

***

'…and that's what happened. Everything was destroyed. I left nothing.'

There was silence.

Jane couldn't speak; it was as if her throat was clogged up with the words she had heard. It didn't seem real; she didn't want to believe it. The unnatural silence seemed to deepen, like a stillness before a storm and inside she began to feel angry.

James swirled round from his passive stance and pointed his finger at Mark. 'It's just typical of people like you, isn't it? You hook onto something and you go at it without a single thought for anyone else.' His finger curled into his fist and he paced up and down.

'I didn't mean to do it,' Mark pleaded. ' I thought it was going to help people.'

'Help? You call this help!' James swung his arm out towards the plant and mine around him. Then he took a step towards Mark, his body quivering as his rush of anger surfaced.

Jane stepped forward her arms out to both of them saying, 'This isn't going to help.' She saw a flash of annoyance on James's face before he turned away.

'James, I'm really sorry, it's not the results I wanted.' Mark stared at him.

Jane saw James stiffen his body as if controlling his emotions, then he spoke with a certain abruptness. 'Bloody hell, Mark, you ignored the warnings, what did you expect to happen? When will you scientists learn? Perhaps you need to stop thinking about *if* you can do it, but whether you *should* do it.'

Mark dropped his head. 'You're right,' he murmured.

Jane immediately felt his isolation and sat next to him. She put her arm around his saggy shoulders. 'We're blaming Mark, but he destroyed his work, so someone else must have done it as well.'

Mark suddenly looked up. 'We have to find the source. Where the main crystal is, and we need to find out how quickly the blackness is spreading.' He looked towards James. 'Will you help me?'

James nodded roughly.

'Do you know if any new mines have opened recently in this area?'

James's posture seemed to relax and he said, 'Yes, I always know who my competitors are. A mine opened about two weeks ago, to the north. It's not far from me, but I really wasn't concerned as they are mining in an area I know has limited crystal formations.'

'How do you know that?' Jane asked, curious.

James shook his head from side to side. 'My dear lady, you have no idea about mining do you?'

Jane smiled, feeling the tension around them disappearing.

'I had a geological survey done on all the area around here before I located my mine here.'

Mark stood up. 'I need to see the surveys.'

'They're in my office at home, but what about this?' James pointed to the plant and his mine.

'Leave it. It's too dangerous to go near it.' Mark paused, 'Is there a way to cover the exposed crystals with earth or mud?'

James looked over the area. 'I can dump some earth from the top. I can also check over the other exposed areas of the mine if you like.'

'Yes, I'll give you a hand. We need to be careful.'

Jane watched them walk down to the open cast area furthest away from the plant. She had butterflies in her tummy that wouldn't go away. In her mind "Spirit Wind", her Native American guide, was giving her a warning. "If the Earth crystal becomes infected, our mother will die." Jane fought the panic wanting to overrun her and waited for James and Mark to return.

It took them over two hours and their faces were grim when they reached her. 'It's bad, isn't it?' Jane said, sensing her question had already been answered by the look on their faces.

'James found more exposed crystals to the back of the mine, they are nearly all black. We've covered them, but not sure it will help.'

Jane caught hold of Mark's arm. 'We have to tell the authorities, Mark. Please, before it's too late.' She saw him frown. 'But the earth will die if we don't stop this.'

James laughed gently, touching her shoulder. 'I don't think we have reached that stage, my dear. No need to panic, just yet.'

Jane shrugged him off. 'Mark, I'm being serious. Spirit Wind told me.'

Mark turned to her. 'What did he say?'

'That if the Earth crystal becomes infected, she will die.'

James tutted slightly. 'An Earth crystal? That is pure assumption based on a computer experiment.'

'What do you mean?' Jane asked.

James looked at them, surprised. 'The assumption is, that the centre of the Earth is a single crystal and not an iron ball. You scientists…' James prodded Mark in the chest, '…discovered this using a computer model of the Earth's core in 1995.'

'I seem to remember reading something about that,' Mark replied. 'Was it something to do with seismic data and the measurement of shockwaves going through the planet?'

'Yes, yes, boring stuff really.' James turned away as if the conversation had ended.

'They found seismic waves travel faster north to south than east to west, indicating the core has a directional quality. A hexagonal crystal has directionality, and its…' Mark suddenly stopped and looked at Jane.

'Its vibration would send the infection everywhere.' Jane finished for him.

'Oh come on you two. Let's get real here,' James interrupted. 'The only disastrous thing happening here is, I'm losing money with my mine closed. So if you don't mind, can we sort out this little problem, before you go off saving the world.'

Jane and Mark looked at him in silence.

'That's settled then, I'll wait for you in the car.' James marched off down the road.

'What are we going to do?' Jane asked softly, as she and Mark followed James. All this was above her head and she knew Mark was the only one who knew what he was doing.

'We need to locate the source and I need James's help to do it.'

'And the authorities?' She knew there would be limited experts in the local government but surely they needed to know.

'Look at how James reacted when you talked of a global disaster. Do you think we'll get a better response from them?'

'No. But we need to tell someone.' Jane suddenly felt alone and the slight quiver in her voice was picked up by Mark, who looked at her and took her hand.

'Don't worry. James is right. Let's see what can be done here first. I need to look at the survey maps and then I will visit James's man at the hospital. I want to see how this has affected him.'

James was waiting outside the car and he smiled apologetically at them. 'Didn't mean to have a go.' He caught Jane's hand and raised it to his lips. 'My apologies, dear lady.' He gently kissed her knuckles.

'James, you are such a softy,' Mark teased.

'Ah you have discovered my weakness, but one I can live with.' He opened the car door and Jane slid in smiling.

***

At James's house Mark studied the survey maps. James pointed out the area where the new mine had started up. 'The land structure holds very little in the way of possible crystallised beds.'

'So how did the black infection get to your mine?'

Mark pondered a moment. 'If there's little crystal in the land, it would take a massive infected crystal, with high vibration qualities to send it so far out. I want to go and see this mine.' Mark stood up. 'Is it far?'

'A couple of hours,' James replied.

'And your man in hospital, how is he?'

'Just got a message that he's on his way here. The doctors have given him some anti-depressants and he's coming to find out if I will still employ him.' James began to fold up the maps.

'But you already do, don't you?' Jane quizzed.

'Hmm, no. Technically he broke his employment by not turning up for work.'

Jane stared at him, she couldn't believe the coldness of his reply. 'But it wasn't his fault.'

'Neither was it mine.'

'But you can't… I mean, it's not fair. That poor man has been through hell. I can't believe you would just let him go…I…' Jane let the words fade. She liked James but this was so wrong. She looked up into his serious face.

He cleared his throat and said, 'But I am a good employer so you, and he, don't need to worry, unless, of course, my mine stays closed.' He suddenly smiled. 'Got you going, didn't I?'

Jane held up her hands in submission and nodded. She had fallen into it big time. Then she saw that Mark wasn't smiling. He looked worried. 'What's wrong?'

Mark looked at her, before turning to James. 'The experiments I have done show that this infection or negative energy is passed on through a crystal's vibration and because of this, it's possible that the vibrations will infect us humans. What I don't know is if infected humans can infect other humans. I'd like to have a sample of his blood if it's possible.'

'Already sorted,' James said proudly. 'The doctors have given him his samples to bring to me, so I can assess if he's ok to work.'

'You can do that?' Jane cut in, thinking about all the legalisation surrounding medical records back at her work.

James sighed. 'People want to work and when they have work, they want to keep it.'

Aisha came in announcing to James his worker was at the gates. When she had left the room, Mark said quietly, 'Put some gloves on.'

James looked at him puzzled, then nodded in understanding. 'Back in a jiffy.'

When he returned he had a small plastic bag of glass tubes and some notes. 'I have a small lab at the back of the house. Come.'

Mark and Jane followed James out through the kitchen to an adjourning room. Jane noticed it was just big enough to have a table and chair against the wall and a tall filing cabinet on the other side. She watched Mark put on some surgical gloves and take the tubes from James. Inside each tube was a glass slide. Mark put each one under the microscope.

Jane hovered close by, intrigued at what he was doing. He stepped back and smiled at her. 'Take a look.'

She squinted her eyes and twisted the dial at the side of the microscope until the first slide came into view. She heard Mark say, 'This is the sample taken when James's worker entered the hospital.' The blood cells in view were really dark red with even darker patches dotted over its surface. Mark slid the sample away and inserted the second one. In this one, Jane noticed that the cell's colour had begun to lighten but the dark patches still remained. As Mark went through each slide, Jane noticed that the cell's colour appeared to stay a bright shade and the patches had disappeared.

She lifted her head. 'So his cells were infected, but he gradually got rid of it.'

Mark nodded and then showed James the slides. When James had finished looking at them, Mark said, 'I want to process these even further and freeze them, so I can see the crystal structure in the fluid.'

'No problem, but it won't be ready till tomorrow.'

'That's okay. Now I want to see the other mine. Any chance we can view it without actually entering it in the normal way?'

James grinned. 'You mean sneak up and spy on them?'

'Sneak is a good word,' Mark said, nodding.

'I have the very man and he can be here in two hours.' James left the room to call him.

Jane looked after him then at Mark, not wanting to believe what she had just heard. 'You can't really be thinking of doing this.'

Mark smiled. 'And how else do you think we are going to have a look at this mine?'

'Well, we could just go and ask the owner. What you are suggesting is illegal.'

Mark agreed. 'Yes, but Jane, don't you think that maybe what he is doing is also illegal. He's not mining that area for crystals, so what is he up to?'

CHAPTER FOUR

Jane was furious. 'You can't leave me here, I want to come.'

'This is…hmm, man's work, my dear.'

'James, if you say that to me again, I'll thump you.' Jane glared at him.

'But you are… a woman,' he said politely.

Jane could feel herself flushing, as anger rushed through her.

Mark spoke quickly, 'An extraordinary woman, and one I want to keep safe.'

Jane went to speak, but stopped. Instead she gave Mark one of her looks that said, "I know that, but I'm still coming."

Mark shrugged his shoulders. 'Okay, but it isn't going to be easy.'

Jane smiled. 'I won't be any bother.' She saw James shake his head. 'Trust me,' she said, looking directly at him. He mumbled something under his breath that she couldn't quite catch, then heaved a big sigh before turning towards the door.

They left the house and Jane noticed a Jeep parked outside. A white man, dressed in khaki clothes was standing by it. His appearance reminded her of the typical image films portrayed of the explorer and adventurer, but his stance was like an alert soldier. Even though he had stubble on his chin and a rugged appearance to his well-tanned face, there was something attractive about him.

Jane couldn't decide whether it was the square jaw and firm mouth or the hooded eyes.

When he saw James, he smiled and took James's outstretched hand. 'It's been a long time, James.'

'Too long, Stan. These are my friends, Mark and Jane.'

After shaking Mark's hand, he took hold of Jane's quite firmly. She saw him glance down at her semi-dark top and coat, pants and walking shoes, before making eye contact with her again.

'I see you have come prepared,' he said in a South African accent.

'I hope so,' Jane replied, feeling that she had just been assessed.

He let go of her hand and swung into the driver's seat.

Jane climbed into the back next to Mark, while James sat up front. The Jeep drove out of the fenced compound, heading north, bouncing and swerving along the pot-holed, rough road. It wasn't long before the sun had set and the light faded into darkness.

Jane grabbed hold of Mark's hand, as Stan's manoeuvring of the Jeep became more erratic and immediate; his vision limited to the vehicle's lights in front of him.

After several hours of driving, Stan swung the Jeep off the road on to a track barely big enough for the vehicle. By this time, Jane was starting to regret her decision to go with them. Her back and bottom seemed to be bruised and each new bump in the road added to her discomfort.

The Jeep came to an abrupt stop and Jane would have hit the front seat had her seat belt not checked her in time. She felt it cutting into her chest but resisted the urge to cry out.

'Jesus, Stan!' James shouted, as he fell back into his seat.

'Sorry mate.' Stan pointed out of the windscreen and in the lights stood a large wildebeest. It snorted at them before moving on.

'Well, shall we take it a bit slower?' James took out a handkerchief and wiped his brow.

Jane smiled, she hadn't been the only one scared by Stan's driving, but she was thankful James had spoken up.

'Sure,' Stan said and put the Jeep into gear. It moved on, the speed increasing but slower than they had been travelling. Within fifteen minutes, they pulled off the dirt road and stopped. Stan grabbed a rifle from the floor by his seat and jumped out.

Jane carefully stepped down, her legs felt a bit wobbly, but after a few stretches, they were back to working condition.

'Stay close,' she heard Stan say to them before he switched on his torch and set off. She slipped in front of James and Mark and followed Stan through the bush-land, guided by his light. It wasn't long before he stopped and turned it off. They stood in silence, listening. Somewhere in front of them, where the darkness seemed to be penetrated by a dull light coming from behind the rim of a mound, the sound of a generator and the soft murmur of voices could be heard.

Jane carefully followed Stan up to the rim edge, her eyes quickly adjusting to the darkness. She saw him drop to the floor at the top and lay herself down next to him. Mark and James quickly joined them. She peeked over the edge and saw a small fenced-off area flooded with lights. Over to the left stood a couple of shacks with connected tents and a couple of Jeeps. In the middle there was a small fire with four black men sat around it. To the right there was a metal tripod, positioned over a hole in the ground, holding a large semi-dark crystal that was three feet long. It was pointing down into the earth. Wires from the generator were connected to it.

Stan passed some binoculars to Mark. After a few minutes, Jane heard Mark groan.

'What is it?' she whispered.

'They're pumping electric into the crystal that has the dark inclusion in it.'

'So?'

He shook his head, so Jane kept quiet.

'Stan, I need to see what's in the hole,' he said quietly.

'There's too many people around, but they may have plans in those tents. We can approach from the back.'

'Okay, let's go.'

Jane grabbed Mark's arm. 'Do you really need to do this?'

'Yes!' he replied bluntly.

Stan crawled between them. 'I need you to stay here,' he told her, handing her a small pistol and the Jeep keys.

Jane looked at him in shock. 'I don't know how to…' she paused holding the weapon in her palm as if it was something distasteful.

Stan picked it up, knocked off the safety catch and gave it back. 'Just pull the trigger. It's for your protection, in case any inquisitive lions come round.'

Jane's eyes widened, but she didn't say anything.

Stan led James and Mark down the left side of the rim into the darkness.

Jane looked around. The light from the mine was reflecting in the sky, which seemed to light the top of the rim, but two feet below it, there was nothing but blackness. Even the moon and stars were hidden in the darkness of a clouded sky. She felt alone and anxious. *What on earth am I doing here?* she thought, gripping the gun in both hands. *Why did I fight so hard to come?* She knew the answer. All through her life she had battled with men, it was a hard habit to get out of.

She gave the dark area below her one more glance before moving up to the rim edge. Once settled, she focused her attention on the shacks and tents. It wasn't long before she saw a slight movement to the rear of the first tent and then nothing.

A short time later the four men got up and stretched. They extinguished the fire and moved back towards the tents. They entered the first one.

Jane felt her stomach churn. Had they been discovered? She waited, listening intently for shouts or cries but no sound came her way. It seemed like hours and she had just about convinced herself that Mark and the others had been caught, when the sound of a loose rock falling behind her made her swing round. Her heart was pounding and her hands were shaking as she held the gun up, ears straining to catch any further noise.

'Jane?' came a whisper. 'Don't shoot. It's us.' She recognised Mark's voice and let her arms drop in relief.

They came out of the darkness and joined her just below the rim. Stan gently took the gun from her hands and switched the safety catch back on. Jane took a deep breath before turning to Mark. 'Did you get to see what you needed?' she asked seeing Mark's serious face. He nodded.

'So what was…' she broke off at the sound of an approaching car travelling at speed. Its lights flashed the sky to their left.

Carefully they looked back over the rim in time to see a Jeep screech to a halt beside the tents. The men, who Jane had seen earlier, rushed out to meet a white man, who was getting out of the passenger's side. His black driver remained inside the vehicle. The man, dressed in black trousers and a white shirt, spoke to the men, before walking to the crystal.

Mark grabbed the binoculars and focused on the man. He swore softly.

Jane heard the white man bark orders to the men and they quickly ran to the shack. Seconds later they came back carrying a similar sized crystal to the one on the tripod, but which was clear and bright. They discarded the old crystal and replaced it with the new one. The white man bellowed more words at the men and whilst Jane couldn't catch what he said, she heard the anger and frustration in his voice.

Mark turned away from the rim, onto his back. 'I don't believe it,' he groaned.

Jane slid down beside him. 'What?'

She saw the despair in his eyes, as he said, 'It's Ferrand.'

'Ferrand?' Jane whispered back, then took the binoculars from him and peered over the rim again. Ferrand was getting back into his Jeep, but she was just able to catch sight of some grey hair and the side of his tanned face. The Jeep turned around and drove off at speed.

Stan got up. 'Is there anything else you need to see?'

'No. I've seen enough,' Mark said, wearily.

Jane took Mark's hand and noticed it was clammy. They followed Stan back to the Jeep and got in. Mark said nothing during the trip back to James's house, he just stared out into the darkness. Jane held his hand, feeling helpless. She sensed his motivation had gone and she was worried.

Back at the house, James took a moment to thank Stan. Jane stopped at the door and watched as he passed Stan something when they shook hands. Stan waved to her before jumping back in the Jeep and driving off. She entered the house with James and they found Mark already sat on the sofa. He looked extremely pale.

'Are you okay?' Jane asked softly.

He sat forward, cleared his throat and said, 'We're fucked.'

Jane immediately sat next to him. 'Mark, you're scaring me.'

'You should be scared. Ferrand is going to kill us all.'

'That's a bit drastic, isn't it?' James said, plonking himself in a chair.

'Well, shall I spell it out for you?' Mark retorted. 'The

clear man-made crystal vibrates at a high intensity. Ferrand has this large crystal being fed energy by electric generators. This crystal transmits its power into a Vogel crystal. A powerful, very precise crystal that is able to pull in energy and transmit it out, at an amazing vibration.'

'So, how is that going to kill us?' James interrupted.

'Program a crystal with the intention to heal and it will heal, but program it with negative feelings and it will send out and magnify the negative energy.'

James laughed. 'Come on, Mark, you can't expect me to believe that negative energy will kill us?'

'Yes, it can. Look at what happened to your workers, James.'

'That could be a bug they caught.'

'The darkness in the crystal is man-made. In its raw form it is like a virus. The vibrations of the crystals are transmitting it into other crystals and into the earth.'

James pondered for a moment. 'Yes, but no evidence it will kill us.'

'The plant, James, for goodness sake, it killed the plant,' Mark said, frustrated.

'It could have died from anything, there is no proof it died from the crystal's vibration.'

Mark sighed deeply. 'Then why didn't you go ahead and touch it?'

James hesitated and before he could reply, Mark said, 'Let's see what the tests reveal tomorrow, then perhaps you'll realise how serious this is.' He got up. 'I'm going to bed, see you in the morning.'

CHAPTER FIVE

Jane lay in bed snuggled against Mark. He had just fallen asleep after being restless for several hours. She was disturbed herself, for she sensed Mark's fear and there seemed to be nothing she could do. She closed her eyes and, instead of trying to sleep, she imagined she was back in the meadow where she had first met her guide, Three Wolves. It felt safe and comfortable sat on the grass and the sun's rays were warm on her skin. She looked towards the forest and smiled. Three Wolves was standing against a tree waiting for her. She got up and ran the distance between them. He smiled when she reached him.

'I'm so glad you're here,' Jane said, dying to hug him, but restraining herself.

'When you need me, I will be here. Come.'

'Where are we going?' Jane asked following him into the forest.

'Spirit Wind has what you need.'

Jane sighed with relief. Spirit Wind had helped her before, but she wondered what he could do to help now.

At the end of the trail they began to walk up the hill where Spirit Wind's tepee stood. He was outside sat by the campfire, but stood when she approached. 'It is good you have come back,' he said, his tone slightly sad.

Jane sat with him on the floor and watched as he closed his eyes. The old crinkled face seemed troubled. 'There is much sadness from our mother,' he said softly. 'Her crystal children are dying.'

'Dying? But it's just negative energy, isn't it?'

Spirit Wind gently shook his head. 'Man creates without consequence. This man-made negative energy feeds off and spawns negative energy. Our crystal brothers and sisters cannot contain it. It destroys their essence.'

'I don't understand.'

'Take my hand. I will show you, but you must be prepared for what you will see.'

Jane put her hand on his outstretched hand and was transported into a beautiful crystal point. It was shining and sparkling with soft rainbow light. A stairway appeared and she climbed it until she reached the top where she became surrounded by lines of silver threads. It was stunning and its beauty seemed to flow into her heart, making her feel peaceful and serene. From the side of the crystal came a rainbow mist. It swirled with the light, and silver wings appeared on a transparent body. Jane looked into the gentle face and soft eyes. 'Who are you?'

The voice appeared in her mind, a soft whisper of gentle tones. 'I am the crystal Deva. I serve the crystal and help its healing intention, vibrate into the world.'

The presence of the Deva was so calming and loving that Jane wanted to stay in the crystal forever. She sighed with pleasure.

Spirit Wind's voice came into her mind, 'This is our crystal brother and sister's gift to us. Now prepare yourself for man's gift.'

Jane became nervous and looked down. Fingers of black oil, like liquid were weaving their way up the crystal towards her. Her heart began beating faster as she watched the rainbow strands dull into darkness at the touch of the liquid. When they were completely black, the strands shattered into pieces.

Startled, Jane looked at the Deva, whose brightness was beginning to fade. Black liquid fingers caught the Deva's wings, sending its poison into the veins and down into the transparent body.

Jane reached out. 'No. Nooo.'

The Deva's body became brittle and solid and as the darkness reached her head, she whispered, 'Save us.' Then the light in her eyes dulled and she broke into pieces.

Jane began to cry. Her body felt like it was going to burst with sorrow. The despair she felt was overflowing her senses, and nothing she did made her feel happy. Everything was so black, even her tears, and all she wanted to do was lie down and let the darkness have her. She felt a hand grab hold of hers and then her body was being pulled from the crystal. Outside she found herself in the arms of Spirit Wind, crying uncontrollably. 'I… I…' She fell to her knees, her hands covering her face.

Spirit Wind placed his hand on her heart and a warm, soothing feeling began to lift her. A few minutes later, her crying stopped and she was able to stand again. 'Thank you,' she croaked.

Spirit Wind pointed to the crystal. 'Your crystal sister has died.'

Jane felt the tears in her eyes again, but pushed them back. The crystal in front of her was completely black. 'Why have we done this?'

'Man has not learnt how to create without allowing his shadow side to influence his creations.' Spirit Wind went on, 'Man is just a child, and knows not what harm he is doing to his mother.'

'What harm do you mean? You're not talking about pollution and other stuff, are you?'

Spirit Wind sadly shook his head. 'As an Earth child, Humans are creators of their world. Many do not know what powerful creators they can be.'

'But some do it by accident,' Jane stammered, remembering Mark's story about his energy creation.

'Yes. We have been lucky in the past.'

'So maybe, this black crystal virus won't do much harm.'

Spirit Wind looked at her and she could see the gravity in his face. 'Our Mother Earth is a crystal; everything born from our mother has some form of crystal structure in them. Our four legged, two legged, and many legged brothers and sisters; the winged ones and even man.'

Jane sank to the floor; the reality of the situation was overwhelming.

'I am sorry, Jane,' Spirit Wind said softly.

Jane shook her head. 'There must be something we can do to stop it.'

'It is self-creating.'

'You have seen the end?' She saw Spirit Wind nod. 'Then show me.' Her hand shot up towards him.

Spirit Wind moved away from her and Jane got up quickly. 'Please, I need to see it, if I am going to explain it to Mark.'

'It will be hard for you to bear.'

'I want to see,' Jane persisted, holding out her hand again.

Spirit Wind took hold of it and instantly she was at the mine where she had seen Ferrand. Her body seemed to be able to transform itself into energy and drift into the crystal, pointing into the ground. It was black and Jane felt cold and despair again. She forced the emotions away, making herself see it as if she was watching a film.

She flowed from the crystal point into the double pointed Vogel crystal, which shot her and the black fluid forcefully out into the earth. Jane watched as the fluid slipped and slid into each crack of rock. Each crystal it encountered turned black and sent the fluid out into another. It spread down and up, even sideward; nothing stopped it.

Eventually she found herself up against a concrete, reinforced wall of a military underground bunker, housing some of the most powerful people in the world. She saw it seep through the walls into the water system, and the people inside. As the people became infected she saw some of them sink to the floor, immersed in sadness and despair. They didn't communicate or move, just laid there waiting to die. Others became angry and vented their aggression on their friends and family. Finally, they were so overcome with remorse at what they had done, they turned the weapons upon themselves. No one was safe from it. Men, women and children all succumbed.

Jane felt sadness, guilt and regret flooding through her. Tears slipped down her face as she watched the tragic last few moments of the human race. She closed her eyes not wanting to see any more suffering.

When she opened them again she had slipped out of the bunker and was in the forest above it. Animals, insects and birds were withering and dying; nature's meadows had turned black. Trees were creaking and groaning as their internal weight became too heavy to bear; then they crashed to the ground.

Jane forced herself away, pushing her body off the earth and into the air. She was being carried by the wind over the oily black rivers that were sliding like sludge into the darkening banks. Over the greying mountain tops that were crumbling and splitting into giant chasms; and finally over the gluey oceans, stuck in ridges of foamless waves, with the dead and dying ocean giants gathered in circles of decaying carcases. The darkness covering the land and sea was consuming the earth.

Jane felt her heart expanding with grief. It filled her chest and felt like it was going to burst. 'Nooo, please n… no,' she sobbed. Her body flowed down through the cracks in the land, deep into the earth to the very centre where Mother Earth's crystal heart glowed and pulsated no more. It was the darkest black Jane had ever seen; dull and empty, a nothingness that was cold, hard and lifeless.

'We have killed our mother.' Spirit Wind's words filtered into her mind.

'Stop it! Stop it!' Jane screamed through her sobs.

She felt Spirit Wind squeeze her hand and found herself back at the campfire. 'We have no hope,' she cried.

Spirit Wind placed a hand on her shoulder. 'We are creators, remember.'

She looked into his eyes and saw a sparkle.

'We can stop this?'

'We are creators.'

'I don't understand what you mean?' Jane pleaded.

'What do you want?' he asked.

'I want to save the world.'

Spirit Wind smiled. 'What do you have to do?'

Jane thought for a moment. 'I have to stop the drilling, the spread of the virus.'

He shook his head and said again, 'What do you have to do?'

Jane stared into the fire frustrated. 'I wish you would talk sense.'

'We are creators, remember,' Spirit Wind repeated.

Jane turned to him. 'We have to create a solution, but what?'

'You will know. Take time and consider this carefully, for every creation has a consequence.' Spirit Wind stood, bowed slightly and made his way back to his tepee.

Jane called after him, 'But saving the Earth can't possibly have a consequence.'

He disappeared into the tepee without replying.

Jane turned to Three Wolves who had been sat quietly throughout. 'There can't be a consequence for doing good, can there?'

He stood and helped her to her feet.

'For a star to shine brightly it needs the dark. One cannot exist without the other.'

They began to walk back to the meadow and Jane was struggling with the concept. 'But if we do something for the good surely we don't end up doing something evil as well?'

They reached the end of the forest and Three Wolves turned to her. 'We are whole, a balance of light and dark. Great Spirit will bring balance where there is unbalance.'

Jane threw up her arms, shouting, 'So why isn't Great Spirit helping us now? Why doesn't he bring us balance against this negative energy?'

'There is already balance,' he said calmly.

'NO! How can it be? We're going to die.'

Three Wolves said nothing. He took her hands and placed them to her heart.

'I'm scared, so scared,' Jane whispered.

'You must seek from the heart.' He squeezed her hands and walked back into the forest.

Jane came out of the meditation more troubled than when she went in. Whilst she knew more, it had only increased her fears.

'You awake?' Mark asked softly.

'Yes. Just had a meditation with Spirit Wind.'

Mark turned towards her. 'What did he say?'

Jane told him about her meditation in every detail. When she finished Mark was silent.

'I still don't understand how we can be in balance with this black stuff destroying the world,' she said finally.

Mark cleared his throat. 'I do.' He went on, 'Man created the crystal to gain energy that recreates itself but to balance that something must be destroyed. The theory of the creation of the universe, is just that. From the destruction of the big bang came creation.'

Jane put her hands over her face. 'I can't take this anymore, it's driving me crazy.'

Mark put his arm over her. 'It'll be all right.'

She pushed his arm away. 'No it won't and it's all your fault. What did you think you were doing? You've condemned us all.'

Mark got out bed and began to get dressed. 'I'll find a solution, I promise you.'

Jane turned her back to him and he left the room. Her tears wet the pillow, as she battled with her emotions. She knew it wasn't Mark's fault, but he had created it. All she wanted was for someone to come and save them. Someone who could heal the crystals.

***

It was late when Jane got up and she ate alone. Mark and James had been back to the mine and were now in the house laboratory, examining samples of the plant and black fluid. They didn't emerge until late afternoon and their faces told Jane all she needed to know.

'You can't stop it, can you?' she said bluntly.

James moved to the chair opposite her and Mark sat tentatively next to her. 'The black crystalline structure has been modified from the one I produced; it's more powerful. It's in the plant cells, the water molecules we took from the drill bit, and in the blood cells of James's worker.'

Jane sat up straight. 'So how did James's worker survive?'

'It looks like loving, tender care, dear lady, was the cure for him,' James replied, trying to sound upbeat, but Jane knew he wasn't happy.

'That isn't going to work for the crystals or the other animals we found at the mine,' Mark stated.

'You found animals?' Jane looked at him, shocked.

Mark nodded. 'They were just lying there dead, their cells were black when we examined them.'

'Then we must tell the authorities, so they can do something.' Jane looked at them, sternly.

'I intend to do that, tomorrow. I've made an appointment with the Minster of Health and Environment,' James sighed and went on. 'They will close the mine and do their own tests. It could be years before they let me reopen.'

Jane stood up sharply. 'James, if we don't find a solution, there will be no one here to work your damn mine!' She turned to Mark. 'You've got to tell NATO or the British Government.'

'As soon as I'm exposed, Ferrand will have his chance to get me.'

Jane gripped her hands into fists. 'Fuck, Ferrand! The world is at stake here.'

Mark gently pulled her down to sit beside him. 'The outbreak is still contained here. If Ferrand gets hold of me it will go worldwide.'

Jane looked at him, her heart thumping in her chest. 'I don't understand, Spirit Wind said this will kill the earth.'

'Ferrand has created the crystalline structure, but he hasn't got the one ingredient that would send this worldwide and create unlimited power.' He took her hand. 'It was the one thing I didn't document, because it was too powerful.'

'So we're not going to… die?' Jane croaked.

'Not as long as we stay away from the infected crystals.'

'What's going to happen now?' Jane felt more positive.

'I, dear lady, will sacrifice my livelihood to shut down the other mine, but I think I need a drink first.'

***

'Stupid bureaucratic nonsense,' James blustered, as he entered the lounge.

'Not a good meeting?' Jane asked, smiling as she watched him fight with his ragged hair caught in the strap of his hat.

'Think I'm nuts, they do. Didn't believe a word of my story, yet they still closed my mine.' He threw his hat on the floor. 'Banned me from my own mine, they did! Refused to investigate the other one. Totally unacceptable.'

Jane got up and guided him to the chair. 'Take a deep breath, James. I'm sure Mark will go back with you tomorrow.'

'No, no, it won't do any good. I saw that white man, who was at the mine the other night, talking to the minister as I left. I'm sure he has some influence on this.'

'So what are we going to do?'

James had regained his composure. 'There is always another way, dear lady. I'll just have to take matters into my own hands.' He picked up the phone, 'Stan, I have a job for you. Come round when you're ready. Yes, you'll need your equipment.'

Jane saw him smile as he put the phone down.

'By tonight, this man, Ferrand, will have no more mine or crystals and that will be that.' He wiped his hands across each other.

Mark came into the room from the laboratory. 'We still need to stop the virus spreading. I've studied the samples we froze. The blood, water and crystal structure is like black oil. Even when I input positive energy into them they improve a little then quickly revert to being dark.'

'Can we increase the positive energy somehow?' Jane was anxious to find a solution.

'It would have to be something extremely powerful I'm afraid and I don't know how it would be done.'

A gloom hung in the room and no matter how hard she tried, Jane couldn't shift its weight from her shoulders. Finally Mark turned back towards the kitchen and the lab. 'I'll keep on looking and trying different solutions.'

'Need a hand?' James asked, following him out.

Jane felt completely helpless. She paced the room. *We can create a solution*, her mind kept repeating.

Several hours later James and Mark returned, their faces grim.

'How bad is it?' Jane asked.

Mark sat down next to her. 'The crystals, once infected, die and nothing I do can save them once they are fully black.'

'What about those with only a small amount of black stuff?' Jane asked, shifting her body forward.

Mark shook his head. 'The infection is self-creating, so it keeps growing.'

'And James's man who was in hospital, what's going to happen to him?' Jane's voice had risen.

'I don't know. James is calling him now. The blood cells, when they touch, infect each other, but when I examined the most recent sample, it looked fairly stable.'

They both turned to James who was putting down the phone. 'He's not good, feeling tired all the time, but still wanting to return to work.'

'Work! He needs to go to the hospital and have his blood replaced,' Jane demanded.

'My dear lady, we are not in England. A full blood transfusion may not be possible and there is a high risk of contracting HIV from any transfusion. It could cost a lot of money.'

Jane stood up sharply. 'Money! A man's life is at stake here,' she yelled.

Mark quickly cut in. 'It wouldn't do any good anyway. The virus would have spread to his cells. We are made up of 70% water and this virus completely infects water.'

'There must be another way,' Jane pleaded, feeling the heaviness of despair flowing over her body.

'I need to know how far the virus has spread and if any other mines are having problems.'

James picked up the phone again. 'I'll check the other mines, then I'll drill for a core sample.' He dialled a number and began speaking to someone.

Jane turned her attention back to Mark. 'What about that man's family? What happens if someone is in contact with an infected person, will they get it?'

'I don't know,' Mark answered, looking away from her.

'And, you said it completely infects water, so what happens if it gets to the sea? Could it spread to other places?'

'I don't know,' Mark repeated.

Jane shouted at him, 'You don't know! You created the damn thing in the first place, you must know.'

Mark stood up and worry was all over his face. 'I don't. It's changed. All I can do is keep working to find some way of stopping it from spreading. If I can't stop it…' he paused to swallow, 'then, what you saw in your meditation could happen.' He turned away from her and walked back towards the lab.

Jane watched him leave with her thoughts lingering on his final words. An ominous silence seemed to surround her and she felt as though her stomach had been drained of all food, leaving it hollow. She became aware that James was no longer talking on the phone and when she turned, she saw he was stood watching her.

'It's not his fault, Jane,' he whispered.

She nodded, tears filling her eyes.

James continued, 'He's devastated by it and he'll not stop until he finds a solution.'

'I know,' she said softly, her voice breaking into a muffled sob.

James came across and gave her arm a gentle squeeze. 'Don't worry, dear lady, you have a good man there and I'm magnificent.' He gave her a wide grin before leaving the room.

Jane wanted to smile back but couldn't. The thought of what was to come was too much of a burden. She didn't want this. All she wanted was someone to come and rescue them and she didn't think it was going to be Mark or James.

***

That evening, she and Mark were silently sitting at the dining table eating a meal that Aisha had served them. She watched as Mark pushed his food from one edge of the plate to the other, only occasionally bringing the fork to his mouth. Jane felt the same way; her desire for food had gone the instant Mark had entered the room from the lab, shaking his head.

She heard a bustle of noise in the corridor by the front door and James came in carrying two large metal cylinders.

'Here's your core samples, Mark, I went as deep as the drilling rig would go.'

Mark jumped up from the chair and took the cylinders from him. 'How deep?'

'900 feet and it doesn't look good.'

Mark stared at him. 'You saw it at that depth?'

James nodded. 'And mines as far as 100 miles away have reported seeing it. I've warned them not to touch the crystals.'

Jane saw Mark's body stiffen, then he said, 'And, Ferrand's mine?'

James smiled. 'Destroyed; equipment irreparable; he'll have to set it all up again if he wants to continue.'

'He will. He has the money and time to do it.'

'I have a man watching the mine. We will know if he does.' James sat heavily on the sofa. 'Before you go to the lab, Mark, there is one more thing.'

Mark rested the cylinders on the floor, his attention on James.

'Kwasi has received a message from my local bushman friend. He has asked for me to go and meet him and he wants you and Jane to come too.'

'Why?'

'I have no idea, but he is the wise elder of the tribe, so

it must be important. We leave in the morning.'

'I can't. There's too much to do here,' Mark said, picking up the cylinders.

James stood up. 'Mark, this is not a request or an option.'

Jane saw Mark frown but she could tell from James's stance that this matter was very important and serious. She said, 'We are your guests, James, so we'd be happy to go with you.' She gave Mark a look that said, "don't argue about this", and saw him sigh.

'Okay, no problem, James,' Mark finally said. He then took the cylinders into the lab.

As James joined Jane at the table, her mobile rang. She quickly answered it.

CHAPTER SIX

Fiona packed up her desk and locked away all the paperwork including the card address system she used. The visit from the private investigator had unsettled her and she was taking no chances. After checking Jane's office was secure, she got into the lift with the other girls from the office.

'No more trouble with your phone, then?' Sally teased.

'I think it will make a full recovery,' Fiona countered, laughing. 'I think I was having a blonde moment.'

'But you're not blonde,' Sally said, fingering her own blonde hair.

'I know, strange isn't it?' They both laughed as they got out of the lift.

Fiona followed Sally in the direction of the car park. 'You parked in Patriotic, Sally?'

'Yes. Want to walk together?'

Fiona nodded.

Then Sally said, 'I don't really like going there on my own, it's a bit spooky.'

Fiona knew what she meant. The dark corners seemed to be magnets to some of the alcoholics who sheltered there to drink.

Darkness had already fallen when they reached the car park. Fiona watched Sally get into her car before starting her own car and driving out. She headed out towards St Peter where her friend Caroline lived. She wanted to use Caroline's telephone to call Jane.

Caroline greeted her as she arrived at the door and gave her a warm hug. 'You sounded so mysterious on the phone, you must tell me more.'

Fiona smiled. Caroline had been quick to marry and was already a mother of two young children. Fiona knew she missed the connection you get with people when you work, and was always anxious to get some news.

'A glass of wine will loosen my tongue,' Fiona said, mischievously.

Caroline chuckled. 'Yes, yes, it's ready. Come in, come in.'

Fiona followed her into the dining room and sat down at the wooden table. Even before she had put her handbag down, a glass of white wine appeared on a coaster before her.

'I like this service,' Fiona said, sipping at the cool, semi-sweet drink.

'It's a pity you don't come more often,' Caroline muttered, slipping into a chair.

Fiona looked at her rounded, chubby face and saw a flicker of loneliness. Since Caroline had become a mother, they'd not met more than once a month, sometimes longer and Fiona knew Caroline missed her company and the freedom to chat as friends do. 'I promise I'll come more often.'

Caroline raised her eyebrows and smiled. 'I'll hold you to that. So tell me what happened?'

Fiona told her about the visit from the private investigator and how she had felt afterwards.

'Oh my God, he sounds awful.'

'Do you think I'm being a bit paranoid about calling

Jane from here?' Fiona asked, taking another sip of wine.

'You, paranoid? No. You're always sensible and calm. But me? I would have had to go and lie down.' They laughed.

Caroline picked up the cordless telephone and put it on the table in front of Fiona. 'Take as long as you want. I'll be in the kitchen preparing tea. My mother will drop the children back here in about an hour, so we have time.' She got up and left the room.

Fiona dialled Jane's mobile. It was not Jane's normal mobile number, but a pay as you go one Jane had obtained in Africa. Fiona had written the number down when Jane called to give it to her. Now, Fiona had memorised it for safety. It took a while to connect and then she heard Jane's voice. 'Hello'

'Hi Jane, how's Africa?'

'Dusty, hot and amazing, but you didn't call to ask about that, did you? What's the emergency?'

Fiona smiled, always to the point was Jane. 'I had a visit from a private investigator.'

'What did he want?'

'He showed me a photo of Mark. It was an old picture, because Mark looked completely different to how he looks now. I didn't indicate I recognised him. Also, I think the private investigator has got your home address, from my card system, and when I checked your office it looked like he even tried to get into your computer.'

There was silence.

'Jane, is Mark in trouble?' Fiona probed.

'Did the PI find out where we are now?'

'No, I didn't tell him.'

Again there was silence, then Jane said, 'I need you to go to my apartment and check it's okay. If it looks like he's been there, call me back immediately.'

'Jane, what's going on? Why is this PI after Mark?' Fiona's curiosity was getting the better of her.

'I can't tell you, just yet. But please, don't tell him where we are, or give him this number. It's really important.'

The anxiousness in Jane's voice worried Fiona, she asked, 'Do you want me to report this PI to the police, then?'

'No, he's done nothing wrong,' Jane replied.

'He was a bit of a creep though, I didn't like him one bit,' Fiona mumbled.

'Are you okay going to the flat on your own?' There was concern in Jane's voice.

'Yeah, I've dealt with worse than him.' The cavalier tone of Fiona's voice didn't quite match the butterflies she was feeling in her stomach.

'Well, be careful.'

'I will do, don't worry. Bye.' Fiona hung up the phone and sat quietly. She could feel apprehension in her body and she didn't know why.

'You all right, chick?' Caroline was stood at the kitchen door.

Fiona smiled and took a swig of her wine. 'Yes, just hungry, and what you're cooking smells lovely.'

'Spaghetti bolognaise, your favourite.'

'And yours,' Fiona smiled.

Caroline laughed, patting her growing round belly. 'You must tell me your secret of eating this and staying slim.'

‘It’s called work,’ Fiona said and pointed at Caroline, ‘and yours, is the result of too much contentment.’

Caroline scowled back at her, then pondered a bit, before saying, ‘You could be right. Lay the table, will you?’

‘Is Roger joining us?’

‘No, he’s working late. I’ll save him some for later.’

* * *

It was 7.30 pm and Fiona got up to leave. ‘It’s been great. We really must do this again.’

Caroline walked her to the door. ‘Are you sure you don’t want me to go with you to Jane’s flat?’ Jake, her little boy, peeped between her legs and Lucy, her daughter, snuggled into her arms, yawning.

‘No. I just have to check it and anyway, it’s late and the kids’ bedtime.’ Fiona kissed Lucy on the head before bending down to Jake, who turned his head away.

Well, call me as soon as you get home,’ Caroline insisted.

‘Okay I will. Thanks for the tea.’ Fiona found her keys in her handbag using the outside light of the house and got into her car. She drove down the road seeing Caroline frantically waving goodbye in her rear mirror.

It took about fifteen minutes to reach Jane’s flat. She parked in the visitor’s space and entered the flat with the spare key Jane had given her. She put the lights on and gasped. The place had been ransacked. Every cupboard and drawer had been emptied onto the floor, in the lounge, the kitchen and, when she went into the bedroom, there too. She stood amongst the mess in a state of shock. What on earth could Jane have done to warrant someone doing this to her? Even the bed had been tossed and the pillows torn apart.

Fiona moved out of the bedroom and back into the hallway. As she turned towards the front door, she froze. The man standing there, with a sly grin on his face, was the private investigator. Behind him stood a gorilla of a man. His bald head seemed to merge with his hard-set face, and the over-bulging muscles on his chest and arms, showed through his black t-shirt.

Fear coursed through her body, drying her mouth, halting her breath and falling like a lead weight into her stomach. Everything stopped, like they were frozen in a moment of time. Then, she took a deep breath and was running for the bathroom, the only lockable room in the flat. She rushed inside, slamming the door shut and pushing the lock across. There was no window and no way out. Croaking back her disappointment, she fixed her eyes upon the door, and the tiny lock, the so very tiny lock.

The door burst open, splintering the wooden frame and the gorilla's two massive hands grabbed hold of her. She screamed, but one of his hands slammed against her mouth with such force her lip split and she tasted blood. He bodily lifted her off her feet and carried her into the lounge, where the private investigator was standing next to one of the table chairs. Fiona immediately felt sick, realising that her pain was just about to begin.

The gorilla dumped her onto the chair and removed his hand from her mouth.

'You bastard!' Fiona yelled, spitting blood from her mouth and touching the already swelling lips.

The private investigator bent down, so his face was opposite hers. 'If you scream again, he'll knock some teeth out.'

Fiona glared at him, her anger shielding the fear that was twisting the muscles of her gut. 'Fucking touch me again and you'll be sorry.'

The private investigator smiled the smile of someone who knew he had total control. 'You tell us where your boss is and we'll let you go.'

Fiona stared into his face, wondering whether he meant what he said, but the slight gleam in his eyes, as he glanced away, made her heart beat faster. She realised there was going to be no easy way out of this for her.

'Fuck you!' she yelled and shot off the chair, sprinting as fast as she could to the front door. Her actions took them by surprise, and she reached the door, with her hand falling upon the door handle, before the gorilla grabbed her hair, yanking her backwards and off her feet. She landed on her back and two seconds later she felt the hammer of a fist crack her cheek bone.

The gorilla clamped his hand around her neck and raised her to her feet. Through watering eyes, she saw the private investigator's sneering face and heard him say, 'You're going to tell us everything we want to know.' Then the gorilla's fist came again.

* * *

Fiona came to consciousness slowly but in intense pain. She was laid on her stomach and couldn't open her eyes, for they seemed glued together with a sticky substance, she guessed was dried blood. She drew in air through her mouth, as her nose was blocked by bone and blood, smashed flat against her face. Every breath she took seemed to struggle against a chest of broken ribs. But she was ALIVE!

She listened, trying to hold her breath so she could hear if they were still there. The ticking of a clock was the only thing making a noise. Was it safe? Maybe they were just sitting there watching her; looking for signs of life so they could beat it out of her again. She waited for what seemed a long time, breathing shallow, swallowing down the blood, and the pain that each breath created, listening intently. Was that a brush of a trouser leg against the sofa; a slip of a shoe against the carpet? Fiona listened some more and the clock kept on ticking.

Finally she relaxed, took a deep breath and whimpered softly with the pain. She found her right arm tucked under her body and carefully eased it out, tensing herself against the pain, as it slid against her broken ribs. She knew her right arm was moveable, for they had only broken her left one, but she didn't know how many of the fingers still worked.

She touched her right eye and cried out in pain, as the bones of her middle two fingers ground together. She waited, listening; still no sound, or indications she wasn't alone. She used her thumb to examine her eye, gently rubbing away the crusted blood, allowing her to see through the thin slit of her swollen eyelid. She was alone.

The relief was enormous and she began to cry, but stopped abruptly, for the pain of a single sob was like having her chest crushed. She needed to get help and the contents of her bag were strewn on the floor about two feet away. She could see her mobile amongst them. She reached forward with her right arm. The phone was just out of reach so without thinking she shuffled her body forward. The pain sent her unconscious.

When Fiona came round again, she was laid on her back and able to see through the slits of both eyes. She felt really dozy and it took a few minutes for her to realise she was in a hospital bed, with tubes dripping blood and fluid into her right arm. Her left arm was in a plaster cast. Her tongue slipped over her swollen, dry, cracked lips trying to moisten them, but she had little saliva in her mouth.

Someone from her right side came towards her and put a straw to her mouth. Fiona sipped the cool water, whilst trying to focus on the face in front of her. It was Caroline.

'How are you feeling, chick?'

Fiona could see the redness around Caroline's eyes, which was the only feature on her face that portrayed the worry she was feeling.

'Could… be… better…' The words struggled to get out, but it was enough to break Caroline's composure.

Tears flowed down her face and she sobbed. 'Oh Fiona.'

Just then another person appeared at the bottom of the bed, a policewoman. Caroline turned to her. 'She's awake.'

The policewoman went to the door and spoke to

another policeman outside before coming back and sitting on the left-hand side of the bed. She took out a notepad.

Fiona's attention returned to Caroline who was speaking. 'When you didn't call me, I got worried, so I called your phone. No answer. Well you know me; I began to call you every five minutes. That would have been enough to annoy anyone, even you.' She forced a laugh, then continued, 'When you still didn't reply, I got Roger to drive me to Jane's flat; the door was slightly open and you…' Caroline stopped, swallowing hard, tears filling her eyes again, '… were crumpled on the floor…' She covered her mouth with her hand and cried.

Fiona wanted to hold her hand, but the pain of moving was too much, so she whispered, 'It's…okay…'

Caroline cried some more.

A grey-haired doctor entered the room, followed by another man in a plain suit. Caroline moved away from the bed and the doctor checked the drips and machines connected to Fiona. He smiled gently at her, 'You're a lucky girl. You've taken quite a beating, but you're going to be all right.'

Before Fiona could respond, the man in the suit appeared next to him. The man's young, clean-shaven face peered over the doctor's shoulder. 'Can I question her now?'

The doctor shook his head, as he shone a light from a small torch into Fiona's eyes.

'The quicker we get some information about the person who did this, the quicker we can catch him,' the young man said, urgently.

The doctor seemed annoyed, 'She can hardly breathe let alone speak. She needs complete rest.'

'But the longer we leave it the more chance he has of getting away,' the young man said, edging closer.

Fiona grabbed the doctor's coat with the thumb of her right hand. She wanted to tell them, wanted that PI and gorilla caught, but her body was too weak and it was so hard to talk. Why couldn't they read minds?

The doctor leant towards her.

'Harry,' she whispered.

The doctor turned to the young man; Fiona assumed he was a detective. 'She said, Harry.'

The detective looked at her blankly. 'Who's Harry? Is he the one who did this?'

Fiona shook her head and cried out as pain shot through to her eyes.

'That's enough,' the doctor said, easing the detective away from the bed.

Caroline stepped closer. 'Is it Harry from your work, Fiona?'

Fiona mouthed the word, "Yes".

Caroline's eyes widened. 'Oh my God, was it that PI?'

Fiona confirmed, so pleased that she had told Caroline her story.

Caroline turned quickly to the detective. 'I think I know what Fiona is trying to say. Harry works on the reception at her work and saw the guy who did this to her. He can give you a description and I can tell you the details Fiona told me.'

'Please can you do this outside,' the doctor pleaded as he prepared an injection.

Fiona caught Caroline's cardigan with her thumb and

when Caroline drew closer, she whispered, 'I… need… your…phone…' Despite being exhausted and having pain in every part of her body, Fiona knew she needed to contact Jane. She needed to warn her, they were coming.

Caroline looked at her, as the doctor approached, then said softly, 'I'll come back, you rest now.'

'No…please…' Fiona's plea slipped away unheard and she felt completely helpless as the doctor gave her the sedative. Tears stung her eyes, for she realised that as she slept, it would be too late for Jane and Mark.

CHAPTER SEVEN

It was day break and Jane woke to a knocking on the bedroom door. 'Yes,' she yelled, half asleep.

Aisha called through the door, 'Wake up call. Master James is having breakfast.'

'Okay,' Jane groaned, and rubbed her eyes to clear her vision. She sensed before she noticed that Mark's side of the bed was empty. She wondered why he hadn't woken her, but then realised that he hadn't been in bed at all.

She got up, showered and joined James at the breakfast table. 'Has Mark been in the lab all night?' she asked, glancing at the kitchen door.

'Yes, Aisha has taken him some breakfast.'

'Any progress?'

James shook his head. 'It doesn't look good.'

Just then Mark appeared. His hair, normally tied back in a ponytail, was loose and dangling down his neck. The usually trimmed goatee beard and moustache seemed dishevelled and thickening stubble was spreading across his cheeks.

He slumped down on a chair next to Jane and let his face fall into his hands. 'I can't stop it,' he groaned. 'It's already travelled deep into the earth.' He dropped his hands and Jane could see a watery film on his eyes. 'I'm so sorry.'

She put her arms around him and he responded by gripping her tight. She was shocked by the force of his hug and of the need for her to hold him. There was so much heaviness and sadness coming from him. Mark pulled away, brushing his hand over his face.

'You've been working too long with the infected crystals. It's having an affect on you,' James stated, staring hard at him.

'James is right,' Jane added. 'Your energy is low.' She hesitated and cautiously asked, 'You're not…'

'Infected?' Mark finished for her. He shook his head. 'No, just tired.'

James got up. 'Sorry, but you can't rest now, we have to go. It's going to take at least six hours to reach the rendezvous point and then it could be several more hours after that. You'll just have to sleep whilst we are in the car.'

Mark nodded and got up. 'I'll just go and freshen up.'

When he was gone Jane turned to James. 'We can't delay till tomorrow?'

'No, my friend is rarely seen, so if he says he'll meet us at a certain place, then we must be there.' James slightly lowered his voice, 'Anyway, I think we need to get Mark away from the crystals. Their negative vibration is pulling him down. Did you feel it?'

Jane had, and she was worried. 'Yes, we must help him to get back to feeling better.'

James raised an eyebrow. 'That, dear lady, is your department. We leave in half an hour. Do what you can.' He gave her a big wink and left the room.

Jane stared after him, thinking, *he didn't mean… he couldn't possibly expect her to…* She shook her head and decided she didn't know what he was talking about and went to the bedroom.

Mark was coming out of the bathroom, towel drying his hair, with another towel wrapped around his waist. Jane went straight to him and put her arms around his damp, muscular chest. She nuzzled her head into his neck. He put his arms around her and just held her. 'I'm so sorry about what I said yesterday,' she said, looking up. 'I didn't mean to blame you.'

'I know. It's okay. But you're right; I am to blame. I experimented with it and then left it. I didn't take responsibility for what I had done.'

Jane frantically shook her head. 'This isn't your creation.'

Mark pushed back her blonde hair. 'Part of it is, and somehow I have to finish it. This is my life purpose.'

Jane hugged him closer, a feeling of dread overwhelming her. 'I don't want to lose you.'

He gently raised her chin and brushed her lips with a kiss. 'I love you,' he whispered, and kissed her with an intensity that seemed to hold them forever in that moment.

Half an hour later they entered the lounge with a small rucksack each. Jane had thin walking trousers on with a light tan blouse, while Mark was dressed in jeans and a white T-shirt.

James's smile was so wide that Jane was sure it would split his face. 'You're looking tons better,' he said to Mark, as he got off the sofa.

'Love and tender care works wonders,' Mark replied laughing at Jane's expression of embarrassment.

'Right, we're ready,' Jane declared, deflecting any further comment.

James suddenly became serious, 'Kwasi has told me we are being watched. He spotted someone last night in the bush outside the compound and he thinks they're still there.'

'It's Ferrand,' Mark stated. 'He's found me.'

'It might not be that,' Jane cut in quickly. 'Fiona said the PI hadn't found out anything at the office.'

'I think Jane is right. I could be the one he is watching,' James added. 'Remember, I was the one who reported his mine to the government, and he may suspect that I had something to do with its destruction.' He thought for a moment then said, 'If it was you he was after, his men would be in here now, don't you think? We'll hide you both in the car. When we are on the move, I'll find a way of losing them,' he paused again then said, 'I just have to make a call.' He picked up the telephone.

'Stan?' Jane asked.

James grinned and dialled a number.

***

Jane snuggled down on the floor behind the passenger's front seat of the Mercedes, as comfortably as she could, with Mark doing the same behind the driver's seat. Aisha gently placed a cotton rug over them, whilst saying what seemed like a prayer.

Jane couldn't believe she was doing this. Only a week ago she was at her office, delegating work to others as she prepared for the trip to Africa. A holiday, she had said to Fiona. But this was no holiday. Now she was hiding in the back of a car, behaving like a person on the run. She didn't know whether to be excited or scared. Her hand touched Mark's hand and she felt him squeeze it.

'We'll be okay,' he whispered.

With the rug in place, Jane heard Aisha move away from the door and then James's whispered voice, 'You two okay? We'll be off in a minute, just have to do a bit of distraction first.'

Distraction? Jane thought, *what did he mean?* It soon became clear as she heard James open the boot and Kwasi open the garage door.

'How could you forget to pack the car?' James's yell was loud enough for anyone outside the compound to hear him.

There were a few thuds and bangs in the boot as if items were being thrown in. 'The tent, you idiot, won't go in the boot. Stick it on the back seat.' Then something came thudding onto the back seat, inches from Jane's head. 'I'll be gone for a few days and when I get back, I expect this garage to be tidy.'

'Yes, boss,' came Kwasi's submissive reply.

James slammed the back doors and boot shut, then slid into the driver's seat. He started the engine, revving it loudly; behind the noise he said in a loud whisper, 'You and Aisha know what to do if you get visitors?'

'Yes, boss, no trouble.'

James drove the car out of the garage, stopping at the compound gates. A few seconds later, they were driving down the road. 'Keep down, it looks clear but I want to make sure.'

Jane thought she was going to suffocate under the rug, but the car's air conditioning helped to keep cool air flowing to her. The suspension cushioned the effect of most of the bumps, but the crunched up position was becoming more and more uncomfortable.

'Damn,' James said, 'they're following in a white car.'

'How are you going to loose them?' Mark asked.

'I'm just texting Stan, who is in a small town about a mile ahead. There's going to be an accident.'

'Accident?' Jane said, alarmed.

'Not to fret, dear lady, not us, but the mess it will create will be impassable.'

Jane didn't like the sound of it especially as there would be no pre-warning for her or Mark.

They travelled in silence until James said, 'Town ahead.'

Jane waited, tensing herself ready for what was to come. It seemed to take forever, then she heard people shouting and the car surged forward at speed as James put his foot down.

A thunderous explosion shook the car, followed by a crunching sound of metal hitting the road. Seconds later came the sound of metal screeching and sliding against metal. The noise was so intense; Jane covered her ears against the deafening sound. The car roared through it and, without warning, suddenly braked. Jane's body was forced hard against the front seat. The car swiftly turned to the right, pushing her sideways towards the back door. After a few more sharp turns to the left and right, the car stopped.

Jane held her breath, listening.

'Time to change cars,' James said, exiting the car.

She felt Mark move and the rug lifted enough so she

could see. It looked dark outside the car, but it wasn't night, so she assumed they were inside something.

James opened the back door and lifted the rug from her. 'I'm sorry for the uncomfortable ride; here let me help you.'

Jane slid herself off the floor onto the back seat and took James's hand as she eased herself out of the car. Her legs were stiff, and it took her a few seconds to steady herself before she could look around. She realised that they were inside what seemed to be a hut, and stood by the half open door was Stan, his rifle slung over his shoulder.

James went up to him and slapped him on the back. 'Brilliant work.'

Stan smiled. 'It'll take them hours to clear it.'

'Clear what?' Jane asked, joining them.

Stan moved aside and Jane could see a narrow column of smoke rising above the rooftops of the houses opposite.

'An engine fault set fire to a lorry, which exploded when the fire reached the fuel tank. Its trailer tipped over and its barrels of tar and steel girders have made a real mess on the road,' Stan said quietly.

The calmness in his voice caused Jane to look at him. This stuff was normal to him. A minor accomplishment in a profession of skills, Jane had yet to see. He must have been military trained, but Jane wondered what he now did for a living, apart from helping out James, that is.

'I have the Jeep ready, this way,' Stan said, moving out of the door.

Jane caught hold of Mark's hand. She was nervous, unsure she was ready for this adventure. It seemed unreal, a dream even. This sort of thing only happened in fiction, didn't it? Mark must have picked up on her apprehension, for he squeezed her hand.

Silently they followed James and Stan to a dusty, dirty Jeep parked around the corner. Jane climbed into the back with Mark and buckled up, remembering the last journey she had done in it and not relishing the next six hours.

James showed Stan where they had to be on the map and the Jeep moved off, slow at first, slipping round the narrow roads, leaving no dust trail. Once they had left the town, the road continued towards some mountains and turned from a gravel road to a dirt track.

Jane watched the land pass by, the scenery hardly changing but rolling on and on. Despite the heat and roughness of the road, she found herself nodding off. In her semi-sleep state she heard the voice of her guide, Three Wolves, calling her. She visualised a meadow and saw him standing by the trees to her right. She ran to him and he smiled. 'Did you call me?' Jane asked, as she reached him.

'I had you in mind,' he replied. 'I am glad you are here.'

They walked to a clearing amongst the trees and sat down. The wind was light, yet the leaves of the trees rustled gently and the sun glistened through the spaces between them. The chorus of bird song gently cooed to a silence. It felt really peaceful and Jane sighed.

'What is bothering you?' Three Wolves asked.

Jane sighed again realising that she wanted to cry. 'I… I'm scared. This thing happening with the crystals is so vast, I… I don't know what to do.' She felt tears come to her eyes and slip down her cheeks. 'I can't believe it's real.'

Three Wolves said quietly, 'When something seems too big to tackle, it is best to look at it in small pieces.'

'You mean like a project, breaking it down to what needs to be done and in what order?'

Three Wolves nodded.

'But this virus is so big, it's unstoppable.'

'Only if you believe it is,' Three Wolves cut in.

Jane wiped the wetness from her eyes. 'But how can I believe anything else? Mark says he can't stop it.'

Three Wolves said nothing, just looked at her.

Jane thought about what she had just said. 'Mark doesn't believe he can stop it,' she confirmed to herself.

'And what you believe…' Three Wolves prompted.

'You create,' Jane finished. 'What must I do?'

Three Wolves smiled but didn't answer.

Jane knew she must figure this out by herself, so she thought about Mark. 'I must make Mark believe he can do it.'

Three Wolves shook his head.

'I must get him to realise he can do it.'

Again he shook his head.

Jane thought some more. After a few minutes she leant back heavily against the tree trunk. 'I don't know. I can't think of a way to make Mark change his belief.'

'You cannot change someone else's belief,' Three Wolves stated.

Jane looked at him, remembering what she had learnt from Jasmine and her wooden box. "An open mind leads to belief and belief leads to faith and trust." 'I have to change my own beliefs,' she almost shouted. 'I have to have an open mind and this will lead to belief and faith that all will be right.'

Three Wolves smiled.

'I know this, but why did I forget it?' she asked.

'Fear,' Three Wolves replied.

'Yes, of course, fear feeds negative belief. I was so caught up in the fear, I couldn't see a way out.' She looked at Three Wolves and wished she had his wisdom, then, she frowned. 'I still don't know where to start to change this.'

Three Wolves chuckled, 'You do, you have just said it.' He stood up. 'Time to go.'

Jane groaned, 'But I want you to help me.'

'Only you can help yourself.'

Jane walked back to the meadow with him.

'We will talk again,' he said.

Jane nodded and said goodbye.

A sharp jolt and the pain of her head hitting the side window woke her. Stan was wrestling with the Jeep's steering wheel, as its wheels bounced out of a hole in the road. She must of groaned or cried out, for once he had gained control again, he turned briefly to look at her.

'Sorry about that, are you hurt?'

'No, just a bump on the head.' She rubbed it, then realised tears from the meditation were slipping down her cheeks and quickly wiped them away. She saw Stan linger his gaze on her before turning back to look at the road.

Mark stirred too; he had been laid across the middle

seat between them. She wished she had thought of doing that for the ache in her neck from her head being slumped forward was developing into a headache. She stopped her thoughts immediately. No, the ache would ease and she would be okay, she hoped.

Mark stretched as best he could. 'How long have I been out?'

James swung round to face him. 'About two hours. There's a village ahead and we're going to stop for a break.' He cleared his throat and turned to Jane, 'I'm afraid the toilet facilities are rather primitive.'

'Don't worry about me, if I have to, I'll go anywhere,' Jane said with confidence. She saw Stan grin and knew he didn't believe a word she said.

After half an hour they were back on the road with Jane thinking that next time they stopped, she would opt for going behind a bush.

The next few hours Jane just watched the landscape become more and more desolate. There were fewer trees and much more savannah. The road, if you could call it that, deteriorated with every mile and in some places the Jeep left the road and drove over the land.

She thought about her talk with Three Wolves. Somehow she had to change her fear into something positive. Instead of the crystals being incurable she had to believe they could be saved, but how? She remembered James's workman and how the love of his family was helping him, but even that wasn't enough. The trip into the crystal where she had experienced its beautiful energy came to her mind, but again it wasn't enough to stop the virus. She could feel her fear slipping in, each time she thought about it.

She glanced at Mark, he had been distant, even depressed, this morning but now he was returning to his normal self. Love was the key to solving this, but how? Did she need to know how? Couldn't she just believe that love would save the crystals? Despite a niggling doubt, somewhere at the back of her mind, she tried to focus on feeling love.

The Jeep bounced over another boulder and Jane squirmed in her seat. Her body was not used to the roughness of the journey and the ache in her back was spreading down to her bottom. She leaned forward to Stan. 'Can we stop so I can stretch my legs, please?'

Stan nodded and within half an hour, he pulled off the road to a small flat area. As Jane got out of the Jeep Stan said, 'Keep close to the vehicle, we are in wild country.'

Jane looked at him.

'Lions,' he answered, to her silent question.

Jane hadn't thought about it until he mentioned it. She stretched, bent and flexed her body, not straying too far. She pulled her knees up to her chest and pushed them out again. Someone came up to her and she turned to see it was Mark.

'How are you doing?' he asked.

'Okay, you?' She saw a slight hesitation before he nodded. 'What is it?'

Again he hesitated then said, 'I shouldn't be here. I should be at the lab.'

She could hear the worry in his voice, so she gently took his hand. 'Don't worry. Remember there is a reason we are going to see this bushman friend of James's. We don't know what it is yet but if we weren't meant to go we wouldn't be here.'

His face seemed to lighten. 'You think this trip will help us?'

'Yes, I think it will.' She smiled and said, 'I believe the solution to the crystals will reveal itself and I know you will stop the virus spreading.'

Mark tried to laugh it off, 'I wish I could believe you.'

Jane scowled at him. 'Have you forgotten what we worked on at Jasmine's; the words that appeared on my box?' She omitted to own up that she had too. 'Belief is not required, only an open mind,' she quoted.

Mark nodded and said, 'And an open mind brings belief and belief brings faith.'

'I have faith in you, I know you can do this.' Jane actually felt the words as she said them and knew she was moving in the right direction.

Mark shook his head and Jane quickly said, 'Stay with the open mind for now. Think of this trip as the next step to finding a cure.'

He smiled and kissed her cheek. 'I'll try.'

She pulled his face towards her and kissed him on the lips long and hard, allowing her heart to open and her love to pour into him. She let him go, smiling, 'If you're going to kiss me, kiss me properly.'

Mark grinned and pulled her closer for another kiss.

'Time to go!' Stan shouted from the Jeep.

'Later then,' Mark whispered, releasing her and starting back.

Jane took the opportunity to relieve herself and slipped away from the path to behind a bush. When she returned to the Jeep, she noticed Stan was waiting outside the vehicle, his rifle laid across his arms. Although his eyes were hidden behind dark glasses, she sensed he was watching her. When she reached him, he moved forward and stopped her.

'Are you all right?' he asked softly, gently touching her arm.

Jane nodded, slightly taken back by his concern. 'It was only a little bump.' She touched the tender skin and was surprised when Stan raised his right hand and pushed back her hair to see for himself. His touch was soft and sensual.

'It was just that I noticed you were crying.'

Jane felt herself beginning to flush. Their bodies were close and his touch had sent a tingle through her skin. She diverted her eyes from looking into his face. 'It was nothing, just some emotion I had to deal with. I'm okay now.'

He didn't say anything, but walked her to the side door. Once she was in the Jeep he passed James his rifle and climbed into the driver's side.

Jane took a deep breath. Was she reading too much into Stan's actions? She liked him, yes, but was it more than that?

The rest of the trip was much of the same rough roads and scenery as they had already done, until finally, Stan pulled off the road and followed a sandy track to a rocky outcrop. He pulled the Jeep right up to the rock face and switched off the engine. The intense heat of the sun at midday burned down upon them and with no breeze from travelling, it became unbearable. Jane took a scarf from her bag and began wiping the sweat from her face. She opened the door and moved to sit on the ground against the rock face in the small shade it provided.

James gave her a bottle of water and sat next to her, whilst Mark and Stan began rigging up a lean-to tent over them.

'How long do we wait? Jane asked.

'No idea. He will come when he comes.'

'Who is he and how did you meet?

James laughed, 'You won't believe me if I told you.'

'Try me,' Jane persisted.

'He is a village Shaman and we met in a bar.'

'What?'

James chuckled, 'I said you wouldn't believe me.'

'Well I didn't expect that. I thought it would have been out in the bush like this.' Jane looked around at the barren land.

James smiled. 'That came later.'

Jane raised her eyes in expectation and James began to tell her his story, 'I came to Africa to get away from my mother...'

★★★

'And what do you intend to do with this Geological diploma?' James's mother said, looking down at the certificate with a degree of distaste.

'I'm going to find oil,' James said with excitement.

'Oil? Really James, I didn't send you to boarding school so you could dirty your hands with oil.'

'Mother, please.' James knew this wasn't going well.

'Donald, speak to your son.'

James looked at his father. He of all people would understand his choice, from one Geologist to another.

'Hmm, I understand your concern, Cynthia, but the boy needs to experience the world and why not this?'

James knew it had been his father's influence that had got him the oil job, but he didn't tell his mother that.

'Well I'm not happy. He's a gentleman and should behave like one.' His mother put down the certificate and picked up her fine-bone china teacup.

'At least he can try it, if only for a short time,' his father cooed gently.

James recognised the tactic. It was one his father used on many occasions.

'Then I could help Father out on his new dig,' James interjected, not seeing his father's warning headshake before speaking.

'A new dig! Donald you said this was the last one.'

'It is dear, it's just that James sees it as a new one.' His father recovered well.

'Look Mother, I've done all this training and it would be a waste not to do it. It will get me out of the house, so to speak.'

'I would rather you be here, meeting and mixing with other families, perhaps even finding yourself a wife.'

James sighed. This always came up. 'I'm too young.'

His mother sipped more tea and then put down her cup. 'I will let you go, on one condition.'

'You will let me go!' James snorted, his anger building.

His mother ignored him and continued, 'You go for two years and on your return you promise to actively pursue a wife.'

'No Mother, NO! I'm not going to be forced into marriage. I'm going to do this job with or without your blessing.' He got up and left the room.

***

'You went into oil?' Jane interrupted.

'Yes, to start with, but then my mother inherited the family fortune when her only brother died and told me she would disinherit me if I didn't come home.'

'So you went back home?'

James laughed. 'For a short time, but my mother's insistence I got married drove me to come to Africa.'

'Did you lose your fortune?'

James shook his head. 'My father got her to agree to invest in me running a diamond mine, but it wasn't diamonds I found…'

***

James remembered sitting at a bar in a small village just outside Namibia airport. He had the plans of the mine area open in front of him. Something was wrong. The layout of the land and the core sample that had been used to justify the purchase as a diamond mine, didn't match. He was puzzled on how his father could have missed the obvious inconsistencies. He moved to the door, for it was quieter, and dialled his father's number on his mobile.

'Father? I have a problem. This is not a diamond mine.'

'I know.'

James stared at the phone then said, 'But… you told Mother…'

'Does it matter what I told your mother?' his father suddenly said. He continued before James could reply, 'Look son, just go and be yourself. Enjoy your freedom.'

'I… I…' James couldn't find the words to express the emotions he was feeling.

'I think you'll find something interesting on that plot,' his father said. 'The land formation is unusual. I'd be interested on hearing what you find, apart from the diamonds that is.'

James took a deep breath and said, 'Thank you for everything… Dad.' He cleared his throat and continued, 'I'll keep you informed. Look after yourself.'

'You too son.'

James put the phone back in his pocket, staring across the busy road, as he composed himself. He wished he could have expressed how much he appreciated and loved his father, but that wasn't the Alcott's way.

When he turned back to the bar he found a small, raggedly-dressed black man sat on his seat looking over his map.

'Hey, do you mind!' James scolded, when he reached the man.

'I don't mind,' the man said quietly, moving to the next seat.

James looked at him, surprised at the good English and gentleness in his voice. Under the man's exterior dirty brown shirt and trousers, he seemed to glow. His skin was not black but a deep, rich copper brown. His soft brown eyes sparkled with light and the short, black peppercorn hair was partly covered in a grey cap that looked like it belonged to the local road worker outside.

The man pointed a long bony finger to a place on the map and said, 'This is where you will mine.'

James looked at the smudge mark the man had left and was surprised that it was at the exact spot he had been considering. 'What has this got to do with you? Are you after a job?'

The man shook his head.

'Then why are you interested in it?'

The man smiled. 'It is your destiny, if you want it to be.'

James became intrigued. 'What's in the land?'

The man got off the chair. 'Nothing and everything.'

James stood up and blocked his way. 'I'd like to know more,' he said.

The man looked at him for a long time then said, 'Meet me sunrise tomorrow at the south end of this village.' He walked out of the bar.

James picked up his map and went after him, but when he reached the street the man had gone.

Just before sunrise James was waiting at the edge of the village. He didn't know why he had come, except something about the man had intrigued him. He couldn't see anyone around and as the sun's rays crept over the horizon, he wondered if he had been a fool. He watched the sky brighten and the tip of the sun emerge from the line of trees in the distance. As the sun's warmth touched his body, he saw the man sat beneath a tree to his right. James walked over to him, noticing that the man was speaking to the sun in a language that had clicks mingled with unfamiliar words. He waited until the man had finished before moving nearer.

The man smiled when he saw James.

'What were you doing just then? James asked.

'Greeting the sun and giving thanks for a new day.'

James nodded remembering how good he had felt when the sun touched him.

The man got up. 'Why did you come?'

'I'm curious about what you said to me yesterday and how you could know where I should mine?'

The man smiled gently. 'Can you give me two days of your life?'

James was taken back at first, then said, 'To do what?'

'To walk with me.'

James thought about the work he had to do to get the mine up and running. Could he afford to give up two days to do this? After a few seconds he said, 'I'll give you two days but no more. When do you want to start?'

The man just said, 'Now is good.'

'I'll need to get some stuff first,' James said with urgency.

'You need nothing, come.' The man began to walk away.

James's mind was going berserk, how could he just go like this? He had no change of clothes, no tent to sleep in, or food and water. He hadn't made any arrangements for the mine or informed the hotel. He didn't know this man he would be walking into the bush with or where he was going? To anyone else this would be utter madness, a recipe for disaster, but he felt no apprehension in his body just the need to go with this man.

He saw the man stop, turn and beckon him and,

without hesitation, he went to him. 'My name is James,' he said as he reached him.

'Kumta,' the man said, in the clicking language James had heard before. James tried to repeat it, causing the man to laugh at his attempt. After his third try, the man said, 'You call me Fred.'

'Fred! That sounds really English.'

'It is the name the government says we are to use to communicate with them,' Fred said, as he began to remove the brown shirt and trousers, leaving himself almost naked except for a cloth covering his private parts.

James wasn't sure what was happening until Fred pulled a cloth bag from behind a rock together with a spear, bow and sheaf of arrows. He stuffed the clothes into the bag and slung it across his chest. The arrows and bow went across his back and the spear he held in his hand. 'We walk this way,' he said pointing towards the rising sun.

'Where to?' James asked.

'There is no place, just the journey.'

James looked back to the village, hesitation should have been gripping him, but instead he felt a sense of peace. He took a scarf from his trouser pocket, wrapped it around his neck and followed Fred out into the bush.

* * *

'And that is how I met Fred,' James said, throwing a small stone at another a foot away.

'So what happened?' Jane was intrigued.

'Fred and I walked and walked. At night we slept in the open and every day Fred found us food and water.'

He sighed, as if remembering this experience gave him pleasure. 'He was amazing, his knowledge incredible.'

'So did you find out what he knew about the mine?

James paused from throwing another stone. 'Well, not really. He just said I'd find something I wouldn't be expecting and it wasn't until I discovered the large quartz crystal points that I connected it to what he said.'

'You think he knew about the virus?'

James shrugged his shoulders. 'Who knows, but he changed my life. Those two days turned into three weeks and I would have stayed longer had he not told me to go and start my mine.'

'Amazing,' Jane said, noticing they had been joined by Mark and Stan.

'It's amazing anyone can live out here,' Stan stated, wiping the sweat from his neck and face. He continued, 'You sure this is the place?'

James nodded slowly. 'Yes, we just have to wait.'

★★★

It was after sunset when Fred made his appearance. Jane hadn't heard him arrive until she caught the sound of his soft clicking voice calling James's name. He came out of the darkness, a shadowy figure reflecting in the light of the small fire Stan had made. He looked exactly how James had described him except that, the glow of the fire, as he got closer, seemed to make his bronze skin shine.

He smiled as James introduced him to Stan and Mark, but when it came to Jane's turn his smile changed to a frown and he peered at her for some time.

'What is it?' Jane asked.

'It is not you,' Fred said and bowed slightly.

Jane was confused. 'Not me, I don't understand.'

Fred indicated for her to sit beside him around the fire. 'Tomorrow, I will take you to our sacred caves. There is a painting deep inside, not known by many. It is connected to all your destinies.' He looked specifically at James.

Jane saw James's hesitation. 'You sure?' he asked.

'You have not found the person we spoke of. That is a problem.' Fred pondered then said, 'You soon will.'

Jane thought she saw a touch of red appear on James's cheeks before he grunted back, 'You keep your fortune telling to yourself.'

'Why is it important for James to find this person?' she asked.

Fred turned to her. 'Tomorrow you will see.' He got up and found himself a place to sleep.

The next morning Jane woke to the sound of someone softly calling her name. She opened her eyes and saw it was Stan, 'Sorry to wake you, but Fred wants to leave early.' Jane nodded and slipped out of the sleeping bag and mosquito net. The sun hadn't appeared on the horizon yet, but the sky was brightening quickly. She stretched, easing her muscles gently for they ached. After the long rough journey, sleeping on the hard floor hadn't helped. Still, she was thankful for the thin mat Stan had insisted she have last night, otherwise she might not have been able to move this morning. She looked across to Mark who was just getting up. He eased himself to a standing position and rubbed the base of his back.

He smiled and moved closer to her. 'Sleep well?'

She shook her head, remembering that she had tossed and turned for a while, listening to the sounds of the desert that seemed so enhanced, it was as if everything that moved or crawled was just by her head. 'You?'

'Like a baby.'

'Liar.' She saw him grin.

'Perhaps tonight I can share your sleeping bag and mat?' Before she could reply, he kissed her.

'Thought you might like some coffee,' Stan interrupted.

Jane and Mark took the cups from him and he abruptly turned back to the fire. Jane noticed him glance back at her before he got busy cooking breakfast.

'Who would have thought that James would have his own bodyguard,' she said taking a sip of coffee.

Mark turned his gaze from the fire back to her. 'James is full of surprises.'

'And who would have thought we would find ourselves here, in the middle of the desert in Africa.' Jane's thoughts briefly touched back to her life in Jersey. It seemed to be another lifetime, now. 'I hope we learn something to help you find a cure for the crystals.'

'Well, I'm not holding my breath,' Mark said, throwing the dregs of his cup on to the floor.

Jane gave him a stern look.

'But I'm keeping an open mind,' he said quickly.

'Breakfast is up!' Stan shouted.

CHAPTER EIGHT

The sun had only been up an hour, yet Jane could feel its warmth already. They were walking across the savannah following Fred. Jane could see why James had been so taken by him, for Fred walked with the confidence and assurance of a man with no need to prove himself. His voice was like a soft whisper, whose words soothed the emotions and his face was that of an innocent child, with lively, sparkling eyes. Being in his presence brought peacefulness.

Jane adjusted her backpack, pulled her hat down on her head and caught up with Mark. He smiled, 'How are you doing?'

'Okay, I'm intrigued about who this person is that James is supposed to meet.'

'So is James,' Mark reflected. 'He told me last night that during his walk with Fred, all those years ago, Fred had told him many things, that have since occurred. The man's knowing is weird.'

'So you think he could help us with the crystals?'

Mark shrugged his shoulders, then said, 'I hope so.'

Fred stopped abruptly and everyone fell silent. Jane sensed something moving in the savannah grassland to the left. First she saw the tips of two brown ears before the head of a lioness popped up. She had been lying invisible on the ground.

Jane heard a soft step behind her and saw the tip of Stan's rifle swing into her peripheral vision. Fred raised his hand as if sensing what Stan was doing. Jane held her breath, her eyes fixed on the lioness, who seemed to be staring back at her.

There was further movement to the right of the lioness and another head came up. A young male this time and behind him appeared the head of another lioness. Fred quietly and slowly stepped to the right, murmuring something in a soft voice. Jane and the others followed him. The lions watched for a few more moments, then flopped back down as if the effort of looking at them was too tiring. Jane released her breath. Her heart was pounding with excitement and fear. It had been a sharp reminder to her that she was travelling though the home of wild animals. She was glad to have Stan with his gun, yet being with Fred made her feel completely safe.

'That was amazing,' she said to Fred, when they were far enough away. 'What were you saying?'

Fred smiled, 'I was telling them we meant no harm and we were sorry to disturb their sleep.'

'Were you not worried they would attack us?'

'Lions will only attack if their young are threatened or they are really hungry. Rarely will they attack humans.' He looked closely at her and said, 'We shall rest soon. It is still a few more hours of walking before we reach the mountain.'

Jane nodded. The increasing heat of the sun was becoming a struggle for her and it hadn't even reached midday, but she was determined to carry on. After another hour's walk, Fred found the only tree for miles and they stopped under it. Stan and Mark rigged up some additional shade and they sat together resting. Jane now understood why so many of the African people just sat under trees or against shaded rocks, drinking tea or water. It was so hot in the middle of the day, that to do anything physical was inviting serious problems. She lay on the ground under a mosquito net, which Stan had rigged up for her, and rested.

Late afternoon they set off again and it was just before sunset when they reached the mountain. Fred guided them into the entrance of a large cave. Jane dropped her rucksack and sat down on a small clump of rock just inside the mouth of the cave. The cool air bathed her hot skin, bringing pleasant relief. She took the bottle of water Mark offered her and drank until half of it had gone. She handed it back. Mark slipped off his rucksack and sat down next to her.

James and Stan did the same. She looked at the men's three bulging rucksacks and then looked at Fred, who was resting nearby with only his small bag, bow and arrows, and spear. Something inside of her, an ancient memory perhaps, longed to be free, to return to the old ways. Jane realised, even as she thought it, that it would not be possible for her now. She liked her soft bed, the air conditioning, the available food at the supermarket and water on tap.

'Have we time to see the painting before we make camp for the night?' James asked.

Fred nodded. 'It is deep inside, you will need to bring light.'

Stan unpacked four torches and Jane turned to watch Fred, waiting for him to create a fire on a stick, but he just put his hand into his bag and pulled out his own torch. Jane smiled, the old was embracing the new and she liked it. She opened her rucksack and put on a jumper, noticing that the others were doing the same.

Fred led the way down a small passageway, leading deep into the cave. The temperature became colder the deeper they went and Jane shivered despite the jumper. The passage opened up into a small cavern, where Fred pointed out small patches of artwork on the cave walls. They showed stick men with spears, and bows and arrows, chasing herds of antelope. Other pictures showed elephants and rhino, and stick women with children sat in a circle near huts.

'Which one is it?' James asked, his voice seeming loud and echoing in the cave.

'We go on further,' Fred said, pointing to a dark corner. 'This is where most people stop.' His torchlight shimmered on the glassy wet-looking walls, illuminating a small hole behind a large boulder. The hole was only a few feet wide and high, leading into a tunnel of the same width. It was just big enough for a slim man or woman to crawl through.

'How far do we have to crawl?' Mark said, peering in and shinning his torch over the rock walls. 'And is it safe?'

'Very safe,' Fred replied, 'a natural passage, not too long. Follow me.' Fred's slim body slipped into the tunnel with ease and he wiggled his way along it, like a snake slithering over sand. James followed him, then Mark. Jane hesitated, watching as Mark's feet disappeared round a corner out of sight.

'You don't need to go,' Stan said quietly, stepping close to her.

'But I want to see it.'

'I can take a photo of it for you.' Stan held up a small digital camera, so Jane could see it in the light.

She shook her head, she had come this far and a small tunnel wasn't going to stop her now. 'I'll give it a go,' she said firmly and slid into the hole. The rocky floor was surprisingly smooth and extremely cold. A feeling of damp soaked through her jumper into her blouse and as she wiggled along, her sleeves rode up allowing the coldness to touch the bare skin on her arms. The darkness of the tunnel seemed to press in around her, but she concentrated on keeping her head from banging against the rock above and focused on what was before her in the torchlight. The tunnel seemed to be a space between two massive boulders that had been wedged apart by smaller rocks trapped between them. It was just wide enough to stomach crawl and Jane felt like a worm as she pulled and pushed herself forward.

Fortunately, the tunnel was short and it wasn't long before she could see Mark's face peering at her at the end of the tunnel. He took her under the arms and pulled her out of the hole, gently lifting her down to the floor. For a few seconds she just held him, then the sight before her captured her attention. She let him go, her eyes focused on James and Fred's torchlights, shining up to the ceiling of a massive cavern. They illuminated long, sweeping, smooth layers of rocks, which softly curved in a spiral pattern. The cavern's walls gently merged with the roof and flowed in a seamless pattern down to the floor, where large holes, carved by ancient flowing water, plummeted deep into the earth.

'It's beautiful,' she whispered, moving towards James.

'This hasn't been seen by many people, that's for sure,' James replied.

Stan and Mark joined her and they followed Fred to the far side of the cavern where in the light of their torches, Fred pointed out the painting. It was of five stick people, four were on a ledge of some kind and a fifth seemed to have dropped off the ledge onto some pointed boulders that were dark in colour. One of the four on the ledge, closest to the fifth person, was holding what seemed like a lightning bolt.

'What does it mean?' James asked Fred.

Fred didn't answer, but looked at Jane.

'Maybe we need to interpret what we see in the picture, ourselves,' she said, noticing Fred's slight head nod. Jane stared hard at the picture and nothing was coming, but as she eased back, her eyes focused on the pointed dark boulders. 'These are the crystals, aren't they?' She paused, glancing at Fred and he gave her another head nod. 'And these four people are us.' Her eyes focused on the fifth. 'Is the fifth one you, Fred?'

He shook his head. 'It is the one that is missing.'

'And what is this person doing? It looks like he or she has fallen into a ravine.' Jane became silent as her mind caught up with what she had said.

Fred peered at the painting then said, 'It is not known what this person is doing except that they are connected to the crystals and is happy.'

'How do you know that?' James asked.

'There is a symbol, like that of a half sun next to the fifth person. It means a rising of brightness.'

'Or a falling of darkness,' Mark muttered.

Jane turned to him. 'What's the matter with you? Why are you being so negative about this?'

'Because I know what my dabbling has created and this isn't going to help.' He turned abruptly and moved away.

Jane looked back at the picture, her sight falling on the person with the lightning bolt. She knew it was Mark. As she turned from it, she glanced at Fred and their eyes locked on each other for a second. A hardly seen nod from him confirmed her thoughts and she moved over to Mark. 'You are connected with all of this. The painting shows you bringing down the energy again.' In the dim light of her torch she saw the fear on his face.

'I won't do it again. I can't control it. It could make things worse.'

'But this fifth person is involved somehow, Fred says they will help.'

'Fred says it's a prediction, but maybe it's a reference to what's already happened. That fifth person could be Ferrand, have you thought of that?'

Jane hadn't and she could now see how Mark had interpreted the picture, but which one of them was right?

The flash from Stan's camera illuminated the cave and she glanced back. She hoped with all her heart that her version of the picture was true, for she dreaded what was to come if it wasn't. The others joined her and when she turned to where Mark was stood, he had gone.

As they all made their way back through the tunnel,

Jane's thoughts were on Mark. He seemed to have retreated into a dark place again. A place of fear and she had no idea how she could help him get out of it.

***

After the evening meal, they all sat around the campfire outside the cave. Jane had made sure she was sat with Mark and she was holding his hand. The flames of the fire seemed to draw everyone's attention and no one was speaking.

'What did you make of the painting, James?' Jane asked after a while.

'I'm not sure really. What I saw was four people on a mountain ledge. They could have been calling up to their gods. The fifth person had fallen off the ledge. He or she may have been an offering or sacrifice. I haven't made my mind up on it yet.' He paused and looked over to Fred. 'But I know and trust Fred and if he says it is a sign of what is to come, then I believe him.'

Jane looked at Stan and he laughed. 'Do you really want to know what I think?'

Jane nodded.

'Well there's four people on a ledge and one has fallen over the edge on to rocks. Of the four people left, one has been struck by lightning. Now the question is, was the fifth one pushed or did he jump? Maybe they were sacrificing themselves to their god, who knows.'

Jane smiled, she liked Stan's straightforward manner, but she didn't think he was right either. She looked at Fred. 'What did you see, Fred?'

'The stone people are rising up, they are in darkness. There are four friends, all joined in some way to the fifth, who is connected to the crystal people.'

Jane waited, then when Fred didn't continue she said, 'But what do you see happening?'

Fred smiled gently. 'That is unknown, but a great force will be called upon.'

Jane felt Mark's hand stiffen and she squeezed it hard.

'So, Mark, what did you see?' James asked.

Jane saw everyone look at him and when she turned to, she saw him shaking his head.

'I saw a picture painted by a race of people long since gone. History tells us these people painted what they saw in their lifetime, so as far as I am concerned, it has no relevant meaning to our lives today. It's history.'

Jane sensed the silence fall once again and a heaviness fill her stomach. Mark's words had deflated all hope she held of finding a solution. She saw his head drop and she knew she was losing him. Quickly she whispered to him. 'Please don't lose hope, we'll find a solution. Trust me.'

He turned to her and she saw the light from the fire glinting in his eyes. He almost smiled and said, 'I trust you, Jane. I always have.'

They snuggled closer and enjoyed the warmth of the fire.

* * *

The next day, the journey back was as hot and dusty as the journey to the mountains had been. Jane longed for a hot shower and a comfortable bed but as it was late afternoon when they reached the place where they had left the Jeep, she knew they would have to camp again. She left Stan and Mark to set up the fire and food, and joined James in saying goodbye to Fred.

'What do we do now, my friend?' James said, softly.

Fred placed a hand on James's shoulder. 'I heard Spirit's voice last night. You must go to the place of Gaia. It may show you who the fifth person is. That is all I know.'

James nodded. 'It has been good seeing you again.'

Fred turned to Jane and bowed slightly. 'You know what must be done.'

Jane glanced back at Mark and smiled, thinking, *it's not going to be easy*, then she said, 'Thank you for your help.'

Fred bowed to them both; waved to Stan and Mark and walked back into the savannah.

'Place of Gaia, where's that?' Jane asked James as they walked to the fire.

'Don't know, but we can search for it on the Internet.'

Stan passed her a cup of coffee. 'Well, the only place I know called that is from Greek mythology. It's at Delphi, in Greece.'

'Then Delphi is where we are going,' James declared.

Mark shook his head. 'I need to get back to the lab and continue with my research.'

Jane snatched a quick look at James and knew he had the same thought as her. Mark's decision was a bad idea. 'We need you with us,' she said quickly.

'No, you and James can do this on your own.'

'I would prefer you came with us, Mark,' James cut it, his voice serious.

'Sorry, but someone has to find a way of stopping this and going off to Greece isn't going to do that.'

'But you don't know that,' Jane said, with some irritation. 'Have you forgotten what happened at Jasmine's? The coincidences and meditations that pushed us towards the truth.'

Mark put his cup down and got up. 'The truth is, Jane, we live in a reality and that reality is, we're all going to die if I can't stop this. Coincidences and meditations aren't going to help us this time. If you want to waste your time in chasing mumbo jumbo stuff, then fine, but you can do it without me.' He turned away and walked over to the Jeep.

Jane stared into her coffee cup, forcing back her emotions. She couldn't believe he had said that, after all they had been through together. The pain of his words was like a slap in the face; a rebuff of what had brought them together. She noticed the silence and glanced up.

James said softly, 'He's not himself at the moment, he'll come round before we get back.'

Stan looked at her with soft musing eyes and said, 'A trip to Greece sounds interesting, if you want company.'

'Happy to have you, mate, but I thought you said you had something on next week?' James said cheerily.

Jane got up and picked up her sleeping bag, just catching Stan's reply as she walked away.

'Nothing that can't be cancelled. I figure I'd like to tag along for a while and see how this pans out.'

Jane glanced across to Mark and then back to Stan, who was still watching her. The reflection of light from the fire gave his face a warm glow and put a sparkle in his eyes. She felt her body flush again and turned away, thinking, *this could become quite complicated*.

★★★

It was early morning and they were back in the Jeep travelling towards the town where they had left James's car.

'Do you think the men watching the house will still be there?' Jane asked James.

He took out his phone and after a few minutes he said, 'No signal yet. Kwasi said he would text me, so I should get it when we get closer to the next village.'

Jane returned to looking out of the window, her thoughts on Mark, who had spoken very little to her since breakfast. He looked tired, his face tinged with a shade of grey and his body sagging as if supporting a huge weight. A word popped into her head. "Hope". Yes, she needed to give him hope, but how? If he returned to the lab in his current emotional state she was sure the effect of the crystals would kill him. How could she persuade him to come to Greece?

The ring tone of her phone startled her out of her thoughts. She pulled it out of her trouser pocket and looked at the screen. The number was unknown to her and she stared at it wondering whether to answer it. The phone continued to ring, its tone seemed urgent and persistent.

She answered it. 'Hello,' she said, cautiously.

'Jane! Oh thank God.'

Jane didn't recognise the voice, it seemed distorted as

if someone was speaking with a mouthful of food. 'Who is this?' she demanded.

'It's Fiona,' the voice said, in a disappointed tone.

'You don't sound like Fiona and this number isn't her phone.'

The person on the other end of the line went quiet and Jane thought she caught the sound of a sniffle, then a mumble of words and a new voice came on.

'Jane, I'm Caroline, Fiona's friend. It's my phone she's using.'

Jane knew of Caroline and a sudden dread filled her. 'What's happened?'

'Fiona's in hospital, she went to your flat and was attacked by two men… they beat her so badly…' Caroline's voice faded as if her throat had clogged up, '…she almost died.'

Jane could hear her crying, then she heard the distorted voice again.

'Jane… they know where you and Mark are. You have to get out…' Fiona paused and gasped as if a sharp pain had gripped her.

'We're not there. We're safe. But what about you?'

'I think I'll live,' Fiona grunted back. 'Those idiots couldn't punch a hole in a wall, even if it was made of paper…' She paused as if speaking was too much for her.

Jane was beginning to hear the old familiar tone of Fiona's voice. 'Seriously, how badly are you hurt?' Jane noticed the silence in the car and saw that Mark, James and Stan were listening intently. Stan had even slowed down so that the noise from the road didn't intrude too loudly.

'Seriously? Pretty bad. In a lot of pain…'

Jane waited while Fiona gasped again. She could hear Fiona's breathing become heavy in attempt to compose herself so she could speak again.

'I know my face needed an up lift, but they did a pretty bad job of it…'

Jane couldn't raise a smile. The guilt she was feeling for sending Fiona to her flat was overwhelming. 'I'm so sorry, Fiona,' Jane spluttered, tears slipping down her face. There was a moment's silence, before Fiona came back.

'Don't cry, Jane. Please don't cry…'

Jane could hear the sobs coming from Fiona and it made her cry even more. Finally she felt Mark take the phone from her and pull her into him.

'Fiona, it's Mark. Jane's a bit upset at the moment, can we call you back?'

He listened, then nodded and said, 'It's okay. Don't worry about it. We'll call back soon. Bye.' He switched off the phone and Jane felt him tighten his arms around her as she cried.

After a few minutes her crying eased and she took the tissue James offered her. They were all looking at her and she noticed that the Jeep was stopped off the side of the road.

'What happened?' James asked her gently.

Jane relayed what Fiona had told her. 'I shouldn't have sent her to my flat,' Jane sniffed.

Mark squeezed her hand and said, 'It's not your fault. Ferrand's men are ruthless and poor Fiona would have been targeted anyway after their visit to your office. They just got lucky she turned up at the flat when she did.'

'But why did they have to hurt her?'

'They wanted our address and Fiona's a tough lady, but she couldn't hold out against the beating they gave her. She's lucky to be alive…' Mark stopped as if a thought had struck him.

'What is it?' Jane asked.

'Fiona's still in danger,' Stan quipped in. 'If they've left her alive it's because she could be of use to them again.'

Jane turned to him. 'What do you mean?'

'If they don't get you at the place she's told them, they'll pay her another visit.'

Jane suddenly felt sick. All this was too much. She flung the car door open and staggered out. Her knees buckled and she fell to the floor. An instant later she felt herself being gently lifted and placed against one of the Jeep's rear wheels. She looked up into Stan's face. 'I don't know what to do,' she croaked, her eyes watery with tears. He gently touched her face, before moving away to let Mark kneel beside her.

'Are you okay?' Mark asked softly.

Jane pulled him closer and just held him. Her mind was full of fear and condemnation. She remembered cavalierly sweeping away the warning Mark had first given her, when he had told her he would bring her trouble if they stayed together. What had she been thinking? She had been so naïve about what that trouble was and now Fiona, who knew nothing about any of it, was hurt and could now die because of them. Why had she done it?

Mark pulled back and gently eased bits of her hair from her face, stuck down by her tears. She looked into his brown eyes and knew the answer to her question. She did it for love.

A shadow cast over them and when she looked up, Stan and James were stood over her. Mark helped her up and Stan leaned forward, removing his sunglasses to look at her. He smiled. 'Got a bit of colour in your face now. You look much better.'

Jane gave him a weak smile.

James held up his phone. 'And I've had word from Kwasi. Ferrand has indeed been to the house.' He held up his hand as Jane went to speak. 'Aisha and Kwasi are fine. They hid whilst Ferrand's men searched the house and are now at a safe place.'

'It means that they will be waiting for us to return,' Mark stated.

'Or they will visit Fiona, again,' Stan declared.

Jane couldn't hide the fear that must have shown on her face, for Stan caught hold of her arm. 'Don't you go worrying about your friend. I'll make sure she's okay.'

'What are you going to do?' Jane blurted out.

'A lady in distress, is my speciality,' he grinned.

'But Ferrand's men and the police!'

'Arh well, I'll avoid the police, but as far as Ferrand's men are concerned, I haven't had a good fight for ages.'

Jane stared at him, the voice was jovial, but the look in his eyes was hard and penetrating, making her realise that he wasn't joking.

'That leaves us,' James declared. 'We'll go to Greece, and Mark, you'll have to come with us now.'

Jane was glad to see Mark nod his agreement. She took her phone from him. 'I'll call Fiona and tell her to expect you, Stan.'

'I'll need something of yours, to show her it's me she can trust,' Stan said.

Jane thought for a moment and went to the back of the Jeep to fetch her rucksack. Stan followed her. After digging to the bottom of the bag, she held out a bracelet of amethyst stones and silver stars. 'This is Fiona's present to me, she knows I have it and will recognise it.'

As he took it, he gripped her hand and held it. Jane looked into his handsome face and caught a look from him that she wished she hadn't seen. He excited her and this was creating conflict with her emotions. She loved Mark, but she was very attracted to Stan. She needed to stop this before it got any further.

'I'll keep this and your friend safe,' he whispered, moving closer to her.

Their faces were only inches away from each other and Jane's eyes were locked to his. She so wanted to kiss him.

Quickly she took a breath and said, 'Thank you for doing this. For both of us.' She turned her head away to glance over to Mark.

His eyes followed hers and slowly a grin came on his face. He stepped back and let go of her hand, taking the bracelet from her. 'James will know how to contact me,' he said, and walked over to where Mark and James were stood talking.

Jane sighed deeply, feeling slightly sad, but also relieved. She dialled the number last received by her phone to speak to Fiona.

CHAPTER NINE

Fiona was lying, propped up by pillows, in the hospital bed, watching the sun slowly slipping down below the window ledge. *Soon it will be dark*, she thought. A tremor of fear rumbled through her body. Ever since the phone call from Jane, three days ago, she hadn't slept. She knew that if those two bastards were going to return, they would come at night. The rattle of crockery out in the corridor drew her attention to the door. With supper coinciding with visiting time, there were always a few hours of frantic activity and she'd be safe, but by 10 pm, the hospital would go quiet and that's when… she swallowed the salvia that had appeared in her throat.

Her body ached with just lying in bed and every movement caused her pain, but she had to keep practicing. She began with her legs. Her right hand shot to her stomach and tears filled her eyes, as she raised each leg in turn, an inch. She relaxed after just one try, releasing her breath in a smothered screech and panting the agony away. *Now the worst part*, she said to herself, placing her right wrist at the side of her hip. Carefully, and ever so slowly, she eased her upper body forward, off the pillow. The muscles in her chest felt like they were tearing apart, sending out tortured spasms throughout her chest. She paused, sipping in air, waiting for a break in the pain. There was none. She pushed on, moving herself further forward. Her arm began to shake under the tension of holding her body upright; her breath was sucked in and gushed out in spittle, through her gritted teeth; and her eyes were squeezed together with such pressure, no tears could escape. Finally, she collapsed back against the pillow.

'I can't do it, I just can't,' she gasped. In her current state, it would be impossible for her to out run or escape the PI and his gorilla, when they came. She began to cry. *Where was this man Jane was sending, why wasn't he here?*

The door opened and Fiona quickly gulped back the sobs and brushed away the tears, taking in deep breaths to relax her. The nurse moved to the bed with her supper and night-time medicines: pain medication that made her drowsy and sleeping pills. The nurse stopped and looked at her.

'You look flushed,' she said, touching Fiona's head. 'And you're sweating. Are you feeling, okay?'

Fiona nodded. 'It's just the pain.'

'Oh, you poor luv. This should help.' The nurse gave her a little cup of tablets and a glass of water. Fiona slipped the pills between her teeth and gum while she swallowed the water from the glass.

The nurse smiled. 'That should ease your pain, but let me know if it doesn't.' She took away the empty cup and adjusted Fiona's pillows. On her way out of the door, she turned and said, 'I'll check on you later.'

Just as the door was swinging closed, Fiona caught a glimpse of the policeman sat outside. When she had spoken to the detective about her fear that the PI and gorilla were going to come back, he had agreed to leave a policeman to guard her. It gave her some comfort knowing he was there.

She spat the tablets into her hand and put them in the

small rubbish bag hooked onto the bedside table. They had begun dissolving in her mouth, so she quickly took a mouthful of water to wash the taste away. All too soon the hospital grew quiet and the night began.

Fiona didn't remember dropping off to sleep and she woke with a start. Her room was in complete darkness, yet she knew she had left the light on. There was even no light from the window, which meant the blinds had been drawn down. She lay quietly, listening intently, her mind filling her with fear. She took a deep breath, calming her emotions, remembering that the nurse had said she would return. Perhaps it was her who had switched off the light.

A sound from the door, like a thud, drew her attention and the thin glow from the corridor, seeping under the door, highlighted what seemed like the side of a shoe. She blinked and focused again. Someone was standing against the wall, she was sure of it. Keeping her eyes fixed on the shoe, her right hand cautiously moved over her body to the left side of the bed searching for the light switch.

It wasn't there.

She turned her head, just catching the smell of stale cigarette smoke. A voice said, 'Is this what you're looking for, honey?' The light came on and she found herself staring into the sneering grin of the PI.

Fiona threw herself over to the right and off the bed. The pain of impacting the floor intensified the pain in her chest and sent shock waves through her plastered left arm. She screamed in agony and would have lost consciousness except for the fact the PI had followed her over the bed and was now straddling her, forcing his bony fingers into her face and over her mouth immediately choking her quiet. He leaned in towards her, his right knee shifting so it eased down onto her chest. A yellow-stained, toothy grin spread across his face when Fiona cringed in pain. He forced her head to the right and she saw a pool of blood, creeping across the floor towards her, from the body of the policeman. His throat cut by the PI's gorilla, now standing over him.

She felt the PI's warm breath in her ear. 'Are you ready to die?' he hissed.

Fiona closed her eyes; she knew there was nothing she could do.

The sound of the door crashing against the wall vibrated across the floor and Fiona's eyes opened in time to see a flash of movement, of what looked like a figure of a man, smash into the PI's gorilla. The force of the impact sent them both toppling over the policeman's body and the gorilla crunched into the windowsill before sliding, unconscious, to the floor.

The PI was startled, but quick, he let go of Fiona's head and pushed his hand into his jacket. He began to rise off her chest, pulling out a gun. Fiona knew her rescuer would have no chance to defend himself. She swung her right hand up, steeling herself for the pain and forced her strapped up, broken fingers in between the PI's legs with as much force as she could. His screech was like that of a fighting cat and he turned on her, the gun coming down towards her head.

Fiona watched it play out as if in slow motion, numb to the pain in her hand and body. Her rescuer had taken advantage of the distraction and he caught the PI's head from behind, twisting it with such force that Fiona heard it snap. The PI fell towards her, but was caught by the man and thrown over to the side. The gun slipped from the PI's hand and landed on the floor by her side.

She saw her rescuer clearly for the first time. A man with a muscular body, dressed in black, wearing a black balaclava, so only his beautiful copper brown eyes showed through. Before she could speak, a thick arm swung round the man's neck pulling him up and back. The PI's gorilla had him in a choking grip and she could see her rescuer's eyes bulging with the pressure being put on his head. She didn't know how her rescuer did it, for it happened so fast, but he seemed to bounce backwards, forcing the gorilla against the wall. She heard a grunt and then they were fighting face-to-face; their fists pounding into each other and their bodies buckling with each impact, until they fell against the bed, locked in each other's grip. The bed screeched across the floor, until it reached the wall by the door. They fell to the floor out of her sight. She could still hear the grunts and groans as they continued to fight, until finally there was a gasping sound and scuffling, as if legs were fraying about on the floor. A few seconds later, it was quiet.

Fiona readied herself, sure in her mind that the gorilla was coming to finish her off. She saw the PI's gun next to her and grabbed it, swinging it round as her peripheral vision caught sight of a figure coming towards her. She stopped, her eyes filling with tears, as she recognised it was her rescuer. He knelt down and gently took the gun from her. His eyes crinkled, as if he was smiling under the balaclava and when he pulled it off, Fiona saw the dark-blond haired, handsome man who had saved her. Blood was trickling down from a cut across his right eyebrow and his left cheek looked red and sore. He held up a bracelet and said quietly, 'Don't think I need this to clarify who I am.'

'Stan?' Fiona whispered and began to cry.

'Shall we get out of here?' he asked, slipping his arms under her and lifting her up. 'Sorry if I'm hurting you,' he whispered into her ear, as she stifled a moan.

She snuggled her head into his neck and said, 'Thank you, thank you so much.' Then slipped into unconsciousness.

CHAPTER TEN

Jane dropped her rucksack on the hotel bed in Delphi and drew the curtains. She was exhausted and so needed something to eat. The journey from Africa had been long. They had decided to travel first by air to Tangiers, which took ten hours, then by road using a Nissan four by four, borrowed from a friend of Stan's. Once they were in Europe, they drove to Greece. Even so, it had taken them three days to cover the 2,579 miles to Delphi.

She felt Mark's arms slip around her and his lips touch her neck. 'How are you doing?' he whispered.

She turned and snuggled into his chest, enjoying the warmth and comfort it gave her. He kissed the top of her head and she looked up.

'I didn't expect this,' she said softly. When she saw him frown, she quickly added, 'The violence I mean, and being on the run from this man, Ferrand.' She moved away and sat on the bed. 'I was so naive, Mark, I just didn't think this sort of thing happened in real life, and I didn't expect it to happen to me.'

Mark came and sat next to her. 'Do you regret your decision to stay with me?'

Jane turned to him, shocked by his words. 'No, not at all.' She took his face in her hands. 'I love you. I don't want to be anywhere else.' She gently kissed him.

Mark kissed her back, then put his arm around her, drawing her closer so her head rested against his chest. 'I'm so glad you are here. I don't think I could have done this without you.' There was a moment of silence before he said, 'I confess that I wasn't expecting Ferrand to be so violent.' He paused as if remembering something. 'I have been hiding from him for years and in all of that time, he didn't touch my family until a few months ago, when he poisoned my mother.'

'So why is he resorting to doing this now?' Jane eased away so she could look at his face.

Mark thought for a while. 'I think it must be because he can't get the energy. He found out how to create the crystal, but something must have gone wrong, because it's not behaving in the way my experiments did. He knows I have the answers, but until now, he wasn't desperate for it. I knew he was a ruthless business man, but I didn't think he would go so far as to kill for it.' Mark shook his head.

'I can't stop thinking about Fiona. She had nothing to do with you, yet look what they did.' Jane caught hold of Mark's arm. 'Your family, you have to warn them.'

Mark looked at her and she saw a deep sadness in his face. 'I've tried. My father is no longer responding to our Internet link and, as for my ex-wife, well, I've no idea where she is. My father was my contact with the children, but when my mother took ill, they disappeared.'

Jane felt a rush of panic fill her stomach. 'We have to find them, we must protect your family.' She felt him take her hand and squeeze it. His voice was calm. 'Easy now, I'm sure my parents are safe. My father said he was going to take my mother away and I expect he hasn't got an Internet connection where he is. As for my children…' He gave a short laugh. 'You don't know my ex-wife, but I can assure you, she has them safe, even from me.'

She saw his smile drop and the sadness return. 'The only one I am worried about, is you. I love you so much, I couldn't bear it if you were to get hurt.'

Jane snuggled into him, squeezing him tight. 'And I couldn't bear not being here, with you,' she said softly. He caught her under the chin with his hand and lifted her head. His lips pressed on her, with an intensity that reinforced his love for her.

There was a knock on the door. Mark eased away to go and open it. It was James, who blustered into the room, looking like he was desperate to relay something. He held up his mobile and said breathlessly, 'Just got a call from Stan.'

Jane stood up. 'Fiona?' she asked, nervously, her stomach tightening, expecting the worst.

'She's safe. Stan has her.'

Jane gave a big sigh and sat down again. She didn't know what she would have done if something had happened to Fiona.

'But!' James continued, 'A policeman died before Stan could stop it.'

The room was silent. Jane placed a hand over her mouth. 'A death,' she whispered through her fingers.

'Well, actually, there were three,' James said frankly.

'Three!' Jane shouted, hardly wanting to believe she was hearing correctly.

'The other two were Ferrand's men,' James said, without emotion.

There was another moment of silence, before Mark said, 'That means we'll have the police after us as well.'

'Not necessarily,' James answered. 'Stan says he has dealt with it.'

'How?'

'Well, not really sure, he didn't elaborate. He just said, he'll keep in touch and we'll see him soon.'

Three deaths! Jane's mind was reeling with the thought, yet despite being shocked, she felt detached emotionally. She was almost glad that Ferrand's men got what they deserved and she was happy Fiona was okay. The only hint of regret she felt was for the poor policeman. If Stan, hadn't been there… She shut the thought from her mind. 'Where on earth did you find him, James?' she asked, torn between being intrigued and extremely worried.

'Hmm, that's another long story, that will have to wait. I'm famished so let's go eat.'

★★★

The next morning, after breakfast, Jane climbed into the back of the car. James and Mark were sitting in the front and they set off to see the site of the Delphi ruins. According to the literature Jane was reading, it was an archaeological site on the slope of Mount Parnassus.

'You know, Stan could be right about this being the place of Gaia,' she said to no one in particular. 'In the Greek world, Delphi was supposed to be the site of the Omphalos Stone, the centre of the Earth and universe.'

'Is there anything in there that will help us find what we need?' James called back to her.

Jane flicked through the pages of the book, speed-reading bits as she went. 'It says that the temple lies on the site where there are two major fault lines, perhaps we should start there.'

James pulled the car into the parking lot and they got out. The sun was shining, but the temperature was chilly. Jane slipped on her coat and tucked the information book into her pocket. She followed James and Mark to the entrance of the site. Once inside, they followed the path to the Temple of Apollo. The scenery was spectacular. Mount Parnassus rose above them and across the valley were more mountains. Broken columns of stone and slabs lined the edge of where they were walking; the remnants of buildings and past monuments long since gone. The air felt clean and fresh, and she could only imagine how magnificent everything must have looked in ancient times.

Five, nearly complete, columns rose up above her as they reached the Temple of Apollo. They formed one end of what looked like a large building. There were no walls, but, on the ground, the remains of stone slabs marked the boundary of the outside of the building and the interior walls.

Jane pulled out her book. 'This is the Temple of Apollo, but before it became dedicated to him, it was the sanctuary of the Oracle.' She looked over the ruins and down into the valley. She didn't know how to describe it, but she felt as if she knew this place. Perhaps she had been here before, in another lifetime.

She turned around and looked behind her. Rising back, into the mountain-side, was a magnificent amphitheatre. It was semi-circular in shape, with stone slabs arranged as seats rising up and back around an open horseshoe flat area. In her mind's eye, she saw the theatre transformed to how it looked before, and imagined the rows of ancient Greeks, sitting and cheering as a play was being performed below them.

'So is this where we start looking?' Mark asked, breaking her out of her thoughts.

She turned to him. 'I think so, but I don't think we can go past the ropes around it.'

'What are we looking for?' he asked, stepping over the rope.

Jane quickly looked around and saw they were alone, with no one in sight. 'There is a place called the Adyton, which was a room beneath the main floor. It was the smallest area away from the entrance. Usually in the west end of the temple.' She pointed to a small, enclosed area.

Mark moved quickly and softly over the stones to the area indicated by her. He knelt down and carefully viewed the stones and ground, digging his fingers into the earth. Finally, he got up shaking his head and returned to her. 'Nothing. You can't even tell if it's been an underground room. The floor is solid.'

Jane looked around, there had to be something here. She couldn't believe they had travelled all this way for nothing. James and Mark did the same, but after half an hour she sat on a low wall and stared over the temple remains. Mark joined her. 'There's nothing here,' he said quietly.

Jane shook her head, 'There has to be, we're not looking in the right places.'

'So where do we look?' Mark's voice was edged with annoyance.

She took out her book, looking through it, searching for a clue. Anything that would lead them to a sign or message to find the fifth person. The book told of the history of Apollo's visit; his slaying of the serpent Python (a child of Gaia) and the erection of his temple. She read how Delphi was known for the Oracle at the sanctuary, which then became dedicated to Apollo… She looked up quickly.

'What?' Mark asked.

'I just want to check something.' She flicked over a few pages, found it and read it out loud. 'Delphi and its Oracle took place before the times of recorded history. Its origins are obscure, but dates to the worship of the great Goddess Gaia.' She looked at him and pointed to the temple. 'This is too new.'

'What do you mean?'

'The painting in Africa is from an ancient tribe. We need to find some petroglyphs from the same time, before the Apollo story.' She looked around. 'Where's James gone?'

Mark stood up and looked too, then shrugged his shoulders. She got up and took his hand. 'We must find someone who knows the older history of this place.'

Mark sighed, turned to her and said, 'Jane, I don't think that's going to happen.'

She looked at him, noticing how despondent he had become. His eyes seemed mournful. 'What are you saying?' she asked.

'I'm saying that this has gone far enough. I know you believe in this, but to be honest, I can't anymore. The virus is real, it was made by me.' Jane moved to speak, but he put up his hand to stop her. He continued, 'I originally created it, so must take some responsibility for it and standing here, listening to history stories, isn't going to resolve it. I have to find a solution and I can't, without doing research. I need a lab.' He let go of her hand and began walking back along the path to the entrance.

Jane ran after him and pulled him to a stop. 'You believed in this when we worked with Jasmine, why can't you now?'

'Because it was all in my head then, and what I believed I had done, wasn't true. This is physical reality, Jane, and we need a physical solution. We can't mend it in our heads.'

'That's because you don't believe we can. But what if that belief isn't true? What will it take for you to change your belief?'

Mark gave a short laugh, 'You did this to me last time and…' he stopped.

'And?' Jane questioned.

'I had to concede you were right.'

'So what will it take?' she pushed.

'A miracle,' he said bluntly.

She looked up at the sky and then back to him. 'A miracle is a tall order, but I'll see what I can do.' They laughed and, arm in arm, walked to the entrance where they found James waiting. He had a pleased look on his face.

'So what have you done?' Jane quizzed him.

'What have I done? My dear lady, I have found someone, who knows of someone, who knows more about this place and we're meeting him tomorrow.'

'Do they know the history, before Apollo?'

James smiled and stretched himself taller. 'He is nearly a hundred years old and his descendants were people of this land.'

'Fantastic.' Jane turned to Mark and said eagerly, 'A miracle coming up.'

Mark frowned. 'We'll see. I'll give you one more day.'

James looked puzzled. 'What did I miss?'

Jane squeezed his arm. 'Mark will tell you all about it as we walk to the car.'

* * *

That evening Jane fell asleep in Mark's arms. She dreamt she was in ancient Greece. The ruins they had visited earlier in the day had transformed into a grand temple, with white stone columns supporting a roof made of marble. She was walking up the path towards the temple, dressed in a long silk robe that touched her feet and was clipped over her left shoulder. She could feel the softness of the silk brushing gently against her legs as she walked. Gold bands covered her forearms and precious gems, of ruby and sapphire, were set in rings on her fingers. Her hair was tied back from her face and when she looked down, she had soft, leather, open-toe shoes on.

She heard a rustle beside her and glanced to her right, noticing a young girl of about sixteen years old, dressed in a smock-like dress. It was tied in the middle by a decorative cord. Her dark hair was severely pulled back from her face, highlighting her blemish-free, pale skin.

The girl was carrying a laurel branch and kept her pace so she walked slightly behind.

They reached the bottom of the ramp leading up to the Temple of Apollo and Jane stopped. The cloudless sky, above the temple roof, was a clear blue. Its colour had such intensity it made the white stones sparkle, like diamonds reflecting in the sun. The young girl came close and handed her the laurel branch, before slipping back to stand and wait at the side. Jane sensed that the girl was not permitted to enter the temple.

She began to ascend the ramp to the entrance. There was an eerie silence and the lack of people around enhanced it. She passed through the golden, metal gates into the temple entrance room. Above her head, engraved into the stone were symbols she had never seen before, but somehow she knew what they meant, "Know thyself". As she walked across the beautifully decorated marble floor, another inscription was on the far wall, "Nothing in excess". *How true,* she thought.

To the left and right of the main room, there were statues of Apollo and one drew her attention. He was stood in a triumphant pose, an arrow in one hand and a large serpent in his other. She stared at the rod standing beside him. It was of two snakes wrapped around a staff, facing each other, their heads meeting at the top under a pair of wings. She remembered reading how Apollo had killed Python and built his temple upon the place of his conquest. Because he had killed a child of Gaia, the gods had punished him by making him a sheep herder for a period of time.

Jane quickly moved on to the far end of the room, to

a small opening leading to another room. A priest, dressed in colourful robes, appeared at the door and guided her down some steps to a room under the floor. It felt quite cold and was dark despite the torches of fire on the wall. The priest stopped in front of a veiled partition, turned and, with a slight bow, moved silently back up the steps.

Jane could smell the dampness of the ground, but also a sweet scent, like that of perfume. As the smell became stronger, she noticed she was feeling woozy. Behind the thin, silk-like curtain, Jane could see the shape of a woman sitting on a tripod. In her right hand she held a laurel wreath and in her left she held a shallow bowl, into which she was gazing.

Jane felt her sight begin to blur, and blinked her eyes quickly to clear it. Slowly she lowered herself to her knees and placed the laurel branch she was carrying on the floor before the curtain. Gently she slipped the rings off her fingers and placed them either side of it. Keeping her head bent, she said, 'Great Oracle, the world is in danger. We seek a fifth person and our journey has led us here.'

A soft, almost angelic whisper floated through the veil. 'Seek the Stone People.'

'We have looked, but the stones of the temple have nothing to tell us.' Jane could hear the desperation in her own voice. 'If we don't find this person, all will be lost.' Tears filled her eyes so quickly she began to cry.

The soft voice came again. 'Ancient stones, hidden from eyes, are still dark, except one. The way is unclear. Child of Gaia, rising with the power of one. Light of stones, shine bright again.'

Jane looked up with tear-filled eyes. 'There's still hope?'

'Always.'

The priest appeared beside her and helped Jane to her feet. 'Thank you,' she said to the veiled figure and turned away. The priest helped her to the steps and she caught sight of a huge stone standing to her left. It was covered in raised markings and flanked by two stone eagles. She didn't stop, she felt faint and very weak. Her head was spinning and she seemed removed from her body, so much so, her legs wouldn't do as she instructed. With the help of the priest, she got to the top of the stairs and into the room above. He gave her a beaker of fluid, which tasted like water, and Jane drank it all. Within minutes, her head began to clear and she was able to stand without assistance. Jane returned to the entrance of the temple and looked up at the sun. Its warmth was comforting and made her feel better. The Oracle's words were still in her mind. Now all she needed to do was make sense of it.

***

In the morning, Jane woke with a thumping headache. The pain was prickling behind her eyes and pressing at the back of her head. She would have put it down to the wine she had at dinner, except she had only had one glass. She also noticed the scent of the sweet perfume of the Oracle was still in her nose.

'You look terrible,' Mark said, handing her a glass of water and some headache tablets. She looked at him, noticing he had shaved and was already dressed. She swallowed the tablets in one gulp and rested back against the pillow. Mark drew back the curtains and her right hand quickly covered her eyes, against the light from the window.

'No more wine for you, then,' he continued.

'It wasn't the wine, I'm sure I only had one glass.'

'There were three empty bottles. I wonder who could have drunk that much?'

When Jane sneaked a peek at him, through her fingers, she saw him smile. 'Must have been me and James then.'

She groaned; his cheerfulness was annoying. The bed creaked as he sat down.

'So where were you last night?' he asked softly.

Jane dropped her hand and forced her eyes to focus on him. 'What do you mean?'

'You were dreaming and mumbling in a strange voice, using words I didn't understand.'

Jane sat up, then grabbed her head as pain blinded her for a moment. 'I was in the Temple of Apollo. I spoke to the Oracle and she said...' Jane told Mark the details of what the Oracle had told her. 'What do you think she means?' Jane nursed her head. The effort of thinking seemed to make the pain worse.

'Well, "Seek the stone people" must mean the answer is written in stone. "Ancient stones, hidden from eyes, are still dark" could mean the writings are not discovered yet, like the painting in Africa.'

'That's it! The stone paintings have yet to be found. They could be in a cave.'

'Except one,' they both said, together.

'Maybe the museum has a painting?' Jane suggested.

'Which museum?' Mark pondered, then continued, '"The way is unclear" could mean it's dark or the location is obstructed, somehow.'

Jane gently nodded her agreement.

'"Child of Gaia rising, with the power of one", I have no idea what that means.'

'In the history of the temple, the Child of Gaia referred to the serpent Apollo killed. Could that be what it means?' Jane nursed her head again. Why was thinking so painful?

'But aren't we all the children of Gaia?' Mark said, pushing back her hair from her face. He smiled, 'But I like the last part, "Light of stones, shine bright again", I think that means the crystals will again shine.' He took a deep breath and his smile faded. 'But, this is just a dream.'

Jane took his hand. 'I think it's more than that. I believe it's a message. The Oracle said, there's always hope.'

Mark kissed her forehead. 'Then you must hope for both of us, for I seem to have lost mine.' He got off the bed and picked up his coat. 'I'll see you down at breakfast.'

Jane watched the door swing shut behind him. She hoped that today would bring results, not only for her, but for Mark too.

CHAPTER ELEVEN

After breakfast, they met a young man outside the hotel. Jane recognised him as one of the tour guides she had seen at the Temple of Apollo. He had a slim, athletic body and his smile, when he saw them, enhanced his tanned, olive-coloured face. His jet-black hair was messed up and fell around his head, almost obscuring his dark, dreamy eyes, which sparkled with aliveness. Jane wondered where all these handsome men in her life had come from. Since meeting Mark, she had met one after another.

'Pleased to meet you,' he said, in clear English, shaking her hand gently. 'My name is Antonio.'

'I'm Jane and this is Mark. James you already know.'

He shook each of their hands. 'My grandfather has agreed to meet you. It is strange, I think he was expecting this visit.'

Jane gave Mark a quick look, but didn't say anything. They got into the car and Antonio positioned himself in the front next to James who was driving. He guided them to a small village not far from the base of Mount Parnassus. Jane was surprised to see that the houses in the village were modern. For some reason she had expected Antonio's grandfather to be living in an older, Greek-style building. They pulled up next to the house, which was on the edge of the village, overlooking the valley. They all entered the small hallway and copied Antonio in taking off their shoes. The marble floor was beautiful, but cold to Jane's feet and she was thankful to have been wearing socks. Antonio guided them into the living room. Jane noticed it was quite compact, with a modern three-piece suite cramped between the door and window. Pictures and photos covered the whitewashed walls, and two old wooden cabinets were squeezed in the spaces between them. Their shelves were filled with, what appeared to be, Greek artefacts. A large window at the far end was open, allowing the sunlight to stream inside.

Sitting in a high-back chair, close to the window, was a frail, elderly man. His face was etched with the wrinkles of age and the skin of his bony hands was so thin, Jane could see the veins clearly. He looked up and when he saw Antonio his eyes sparkled. He smiled.

'Grandfather, I've brought the visitors I told you about.' Antonio went to him and kissed the top of his grey-haired head.

'Good, good,' the grandfather said, waving Jane, Mark and James closer.

'They want to know about the history before Apollo,' Antonio continued, 'this is Jane, Mark and James.'

Jane took the fragile hand offered to her and was surprised by his firm grip when they shook. She moved to a wooden chair close by him to make room for the others to shake his hand.

'My name is Demetri. Here, my family, lived a long time.' His voice was crackly and weak, his English, broken. 'They, hmm, priests to the Oracle, in the Temple.'

Jane leaned forward. 'But what about before then?'

Demetri looked at her and smiled. 'Yes, my ancestors,

here at place of Gaia.' Then he spoke quickly in Greek.

After Demetri had finished, Jane looked at Antonio for a translation.

'They were goat herders and one of his family found a crack in the earth, which gave him,' he struggled to find the correct word, 'divine pleasure, I think is the word. This allowed him to see the past and future.'

'But what about before that, was there a cave?'

Antonio spoke to Demetri in Greek and he pondered for a moment before shaking his head.

'Or some paintings in a cave?' Jane persisted.

Demetri looked at her and shook his head.

'Are you sure?' she challenged.

Mark touched her arm. 'Jane, there's nothing here.'

She shrugged his hand away. 'There has to be, my dream was so vivid.'

'Please! Jane.'

She turned at the sound of annoyance in his voice and saw a resigned expression on his face. She realised he was right, she was grasping at anything, when maybe there was nothing there in the first place. 'I'm sorry,' she whispered, dropping her head. She felt Demetri take hold of her hand and when she looked up, he spoke in Greek again.

Antonio translated, 'He says, he has something that might help, he found it as a child.'

Demetri pointed to one of the cabinets and Antonio went to it.

'The stone?' he asked.

Demetri nodded, then relaxed back into the chair, taking a deep breath. Jane noticed that his strength seemed to have left him for a moment. Antonio carefully picked up a slab of stone and carried it to his grandfather. 'There is something on it,' he stated. Demetri didn't move to take it from him, so Jane took it instead.

It had uneven, broken edges and was flat, only an inch or so thick. It reminded Jane of a piece of plaster that had detached from a wall. She looked at the symbol carved deeply into the surface. Nearly all the colour had gone, but a pale yellow and red dye made circles that overlapped each other, creating a middle oval shape. A line ran through it from top to bottom, or it could have been side to side depending on how she held it.

'Where did you get this?' she asked.

The old man thought for a moment, trying to recall old memories. 'I…' He shook his head.

'You said, you found it as a child, Grandfather,' Antonio said, then spoke quickly in Greek. When he had finished, he turned to Jane. 'I remember him telling me of how he used to explore the mountains, looking for adventure. I have asked him if it was this mountain.'

The old man's eyes seemed to sparkle and he chuckled to himself. 'Yes, Yes.' He continued in Greek until he fell silent.

Jane looked at Antonio, who immediately said, 'He said it got him into a lot of trouble.'

Jane smiled.

'Grandfather said, he played on the higher ledges of the mountain above where the Temple of Apollo is. It is about half a day's walk.'

Jane took hold of one of Demitri's hands. 'Thank you,' she said softly. He smiled and squeezed her fingers.

After he had released her, she placed the stone on the table and took out her camera. She pointed to the stone and camera. Demitri nodded his permission and she took the photo before getting up to join the others by the door.

'We are going to need camping gear and a guide,' James declared turning to Antonio. 'Are you able to help us?'

Antonio nodded eagerly. 'To visit the places of my grandfather, is an honour,' he paused, then said, 'we can obtain the gear and supplies in town and be there before nightfall.'

Jane could feel excitement building in her stomach, but also fear. What if there was nothing there to find? What if all that she had seen was, as Mark said, all in her mind? Could he also be right about the virus? It was man-made so a creation of the physical world and maybe only science could find a cure. But something inside of her felt there was something more and maybe it was because belief and science needed to work together. She got into the car with her mind still trying to analyse her thoughts.

The shopping, in the modern town of Delphi, went well and with packed rucksacks in the back of the car and a change to warmer clothes, they drove to Antonio's house to pick him up. He was ready and jumped into the front, guiding James to the last parking area, up the mountain, past his grandfather's house.

James parked the car and they all got out, collecting their gear from the back. Jane was struggling with the straps of her rucksack, until Mark pulled the strap out and flicked it on to her shoulder. He then adjusted them so the weight of the rucksack was even on her back. 'It's quite heavy,' she mumbled, clicking the waist belt in place.

'Not as heavy as mine or James's. Fancy swapping?'

Jane looked at his bag. It was the same size as her own except that it was bulked out with camping gear and sleeping bags on the top. 'Don't think so,' she said, smiling.

The sun was high in the sky and its heat was making her warm. She had dressed in walking trousers, t-shirt and jumper, knowing that the higher they went, the colder it would get, and at night it would be even colder.

Antonio set off up an easy pathway and Jane followed him, with Mark and James coming behind. The rising path didn't seem too bad and she felt confident she could do it easily, even with the heavy rucksack. An hour later, she began to feel the effect of the path's steepness and the rucksack's pressure on her back. The higher they went, the harder her body had to work and her breathing started to get difficult. She was also conscious the path was getting narrower and the mountain edge, to her right, was dropping away to a ravine.

In an attempt to keep herself away from the edge, she moved to the left causing her rucksack to catch on a outcrop of rock. The jolt pushed her outwards and only Mark's steadying hand prevented her from slipping off the path. Jane gasped in what breath she could muster, her heart thumping madly in her chest.

'You okay?' Mark asked, concern in his voice. Jane nodded, unable to speak. She saw Antonio stop just ahead and with her left hand running along the rocks, for moral support, she walked, one foot in front of the other, until she reached him. He had stopped where the path was wider creating a small ledge. She positioned herself deep into the recess and bent over to ease the weight on her back. The air was thin and she drew in deep breaths.

'Time to eat and drink,' Antonio said.

'It's only been an hour…' Jane gasped, sliding her rucksack to the ground.

'An hour, yes, but on this path, resting is good.'

Mark and James joined her, dropping their rucksacks and sitting down.

'How far now?' James asked, breathless.

'Another hour and we reach the first ridge my grandfather told me about, then a further hour should see us there.' He looked up to the sky. 'We will reach it before dark.'

Jane nodded and took the bottle of water Mark handed her. 'Another two hours of walking,' she groaned, 'what was I thinking when I agreed to do this?' She saw Mark smile and heard his chuckle. For a moment all worry of the infected crystals seemed distant, another time even. It was as if they were on holiday, without any cares or worries, apart from keeping on the path. She pulled a fruit bar from her rucksack pocket and started to eat it. She thought about what they would have been doing now, if things had been normal with the crystals. It was hard to believe they had done so much. It didn't seem real to be sat here on the side of this mountain.

'Are you rested enough?' Antonio asked, breaking into her thoughts. She stood up straight and hiked her rucksack onto her back. 'Let's go,' she said, with enthusiasm that surprised even her.

Two hours later, they reached a flat area among the bushes and trees of a rocky landscape. Jane roughly dropped her rucksack to the floor and sat down. Her back was aching, her shoulders felt like ridges had been stamped into them and the muscles of her legs were screaming in protest at taking another step. The climb had got harder after the first stop, with the path disappearing in places, leaving them to climb up uneven stretches of rock and scrub. She had decided that the walk with Fred, had been easy compared to this.

The sun disappeared behind the mountainside and with dusk came the cold. Jane was too tired to offer to help with the tents or to set up the campfire. She just sat against a small tree and closed her eyes. She didn't know how long she was there, but she woke to a hand on her shoulder, shaking her. She opened her eyes and saw Mark. He looked worried.

'Are you all right?'

'Just tired,' she said, gently flexing her seized up neck.

Mark knelt down and took hold of her hands. The warmth of his grip made her realise just how cold her own were.

'You're freezing!' he exclaimed. 'Come and sit by the fire. And where's your coat?' He helped her to her feet. Jane tried to get to her rucksack, to pull out her coat, but staggered forward, her knees and legs resisting her weight. Mark slipped his arm around her and guided her to the fire. It was blazing fiercely and she carefully sat on a flat stone positioned around it. Mark took her coat from her rucksack and assisted her in putting it on. She felt numb and her joints seemed reluctant to move. The intense warmth on her face, from the fire, was the only thing on her body absorbing the heat. Mark was rubbing her hands frantically to bring back the circulation.

'I'm sorry for not helping you set up,' Jane blurted out.

James threw a rug over her shoulders. 'My dear lady, you did a sterling job getting here.'

Jane gave him one of her stares, that said, "Don't patronise me."

He cleared his throat and immediately said, 'Well, I meant that it's quite a hike for a woman.' He stopped short, then said, 'Well, it's a difficult climb for a man and you're a w…'

Jane started to laugh. 'Shut up, James, before you get yourself deeper into trouble.'

'I agree with you on that one,' he replied, relief in his voice. He sat next to her.

Jane started to feel better with the warmth spreading into her body. She took the cup of steaming liquid Antonio offered her and took a sip. It was coffee.

'We shall look for the cave tomorrow. I have a few notes here from my grandfather,' Antonio said, patting his coat pocket, 'but his memory isn't good.'

Jane liked Antonio and knew that if anyone was going to find the cave, it would be him.

★★★

The dew on the grass was dense and the air was fresh when Jane emerged from her and Mark's tent. She had slept well with Mark's body cocooning her to keep her warm. Her back still ached from the climb and the muscles in her legs were sore, but she felt excited and energised. Following a breakfast of bacon and fire-toasted bread, cooked by James, she was ready to go.

They split into two teams, Antonio and James, and her and Mark. Antonio handed her a crude hand-drawn map of the mountain area. He traced his finger over the area where her and Mark were to search.

Leaving the pitched tents and campsite, she and Mark headed northwest, through the shrub area towards some overhanging rocks. Jane surveyed every rock cluster she came to with enthusiasm, tirelessly working her way across and up the rock face; peering down minute holes and across natural rock breaks. She continued without a break for two hours.

'Jane!'

She heard Mark's call and rushed over to him. 'Have you found it?' she asked eagerly.

'No. We need to stop for a bit. Here's some water.'

Jane turned away from him sharply, disappointed. 'I'm okay!' she said stiffly. She felt him catch hold of her arm, stopping her in her stride.

'You need some water,' he said firmly.

She was about to refuse but seeing the determined look on his face she thought better of it and took the bottle. The cool water soothed the dryness of her throat, which she didn't realise she had. A few more mouthfuls and she handed the bottle back. 'We need to keep looking.'

Mark continued to hold her arm. 'It's not here.'

'It might be, we just haven't seen it.'

'Jane, you're deluding yourself.'

She pulled her arm out of his grip. 'And you're not being helpful!' she snapped.

'Well least I'm not going round like a desperate nutcase. Just look at yourself!'

Jane felt the sting of his words but she refused to let herself get emotional. 'I've been right so far. The coincidences have got us here, haven't they? So the cave has got to be here.' She turned away.

Mark caught her shoulder and pulled her back round so she faced him. He looked at her and sadly shook his head. Tears formed in her eyes as she said, 'Remember, Mark, how we followed the coincidences before; how they led us to our truth. Why don't you believe it now?'

'I do believe in them, but I recall that they appeared to us and if we acted on them more followed. This desperate search for the cave is not coincidence.'

'But they have led us here,' Jane said with a croak in her voice.

Mark pulled her close and held her. 'Yes, they have but shouldn't we be looking for a sign to where the cave is, instead of blindly rushing around searching for it?'

Jane realised the truth of his words. She hadn't appreciated how much fear she was holding and she hugged him. She stayed that way for a while, listening, through his chest, to the beat of his heart; feeling the rise and fall of his breath and the warmth of his embrace. The air around them had taken on a stillness. There was no sound outside what their bodies were making. Then she heard it.

It was as if her and Mark's thoughts had joined for they both said together, 'Dripping water!'

Jane pulled away from him, stepping gently back. She moved her head from side to side as she tried to find the direction of where the sound was coming from. Mark pointed to a shrub-covered area at the base of a small, hardly noticeable overhang.

Jane moved over to it, her heart beating faster with each step. Dare she hope this was it? She rested her head against the overhang, listening. The dripping water was clearer and coming from below where she was.

Mark knelt down and began to pull the shrubs away from the rock face. A minute later they were peering at a hole. He took out his torch, moved forward and shone it inside. Jane caught a glimpse of something as the light flashed downwards. Mark turned to her, his smile was wide and his eyes flashed with excitement. His face said it all.

'Let me see,' Jane yelled and quickly took the torch, moving into the spot Mark had vacated. The light flittered through the hole into the darkness, catching multiple piles of column-like structures rising from the floor and hanging from the roof. As it shone deeper inside, Jane saw the hole open out into a cavern. 'We've found it,' she whispered and the cave echoed her whisper back.

'Go and get James and Antonio,' Jane said, getting up from her crouched position. 'I'll start clearing the hole.'

'Don't go inside until we're back,' Mark instructed.

'I won't, just hurry back.'

She saw him take a look at their position for his bearings and then move off, retracing the path they had come on. She turned back to the small melon-size opening and began pulling away the grass and shrubs around it. Slowly the hole turned into a long slit and after half an hour she had cleared the whole area around the rock, exposing a small, narrow entrance, not even a foot high and three feet long. She groaned as she surveyed it. This didn't look like a cave that children would have played in, the entrance was too small. She heard a noise behind her and turned to see Mark, James and Antonio coming towards her.

'I think it's a false call,' she said sadly. 'No one could get in there, not even children.'

Antonio inspected what she had uncovered and looked more closely at the ground and overhang. 'This is limestone build up.' He pointed to mounds of what, to Jane, seemed like rock. She looked at him puzzled.

'The water creates stalactites and stalagmites,' Antonio explained.

Jane shook her head, not understanding.

Antonio took out a small pickaxe, similar to what climbers use, and knocked at the rocky mounds. They cracked and broke into pieces. Before long there was a hole nearly three feet high and big enough for them to crawl through.

'Antonio, you are a genius,' she cried and joined him at the hole. The torchlight showed a small drop to the cave floor.

Antonio pointed to the rock columns that were littering the floor. 'Stalagmites,' he said. Then he pointed to those coming down from the cave roof. 'Stalactites.'

Jane looked at them in awe. Some of the stalactites, closer to the walls, had joined to those forming from the floor to make huge columns. She pointed to them. 'Just like the Temple of Apollo,' she said, mainly to herself.

Antonio looked at her. 'That's a good observation. If this is where my grandfather found the piece of petroglyph stone, then this could have been the original Oracle's temple.'

Jane felt like giggling, the excitement of being the first one to discover something ancient was intoxicating. She watched Antonio fetch a small bag filled with ropes. He took one rope out and slipped the bag over his shoulder. He tied one end of the rope to a small tree near the cave entrance and sent the other end of it into the cave. She held her torch so its light shone on the floor as he slipped, feet first, on his belly, into the hole before gently dropping to the cave floor.

He looked up at her. 'It's about eight feet, come.'

Jane turned on to her front and slid backwards into the hole, holding onto the rope the same way she had seen Antonio do. As she moved further in, she noticed that the rock wall was slippery but her feet were able to locate small jutting out pieces of rock to steady herself. When she was at her full length she heard Antonio say, 'Just over two feet to the ground.' She looked down to the light from his torch and jumped, landing softly. Antonio touched her arm. 'I'm good,' she said and switching on her own torch she moved away.

With the sound of Mark and James making their entry behind her, Jane stepped carefully round the piles of rock formations, her torch scanning the cave walls. She could see no inscriptions anywhere. She turned to the others as they joined her. 'I can't see anything.'

Antonio squeezed her shoulder, 'The ancient people

usually painted or drew up high or where it was very dry, so we look up.'

Jane shone her torch up, moving it round the stalactites; still nothing.

'Over here,' Mark called out and Jane rushed over to him. His torchlight was shinning into a narrow, dark corner.

'An opening,' she said, letting her torch join his. She moved aside to let Antonio through. He peered at the opening and squeezed through. Jane waited, unconsciously holding her breath. Antonio reappeared into their lights and the smile on his face told her all she needed to know. 'You found it.'

'It's amazing, come.'

She took Antonio's hand and squeezed herself between the rocks until they widened into a large cavern with huge overhangs. She couldn't speak, the words wouldn't come, for the beauty of the cave was indescribable. The torchlight created rainbow colours over the ceiling, which sparkled like it had its own star system. Huge rock overhangs bulged out from the side walls. Then her light picked up the red coloured hand patterns forming an amazing mosaic of handprints forming a circle on the furthest wall.

Antonio came up beside her, his torch shining on the centre of the circle. It illuminated the image of a single hand above two vertical lines, resting on a rectangle block with an arrow pointing to a triangle shape.

'What does it mean?' Jane whispered.

Antonio pointed to the vertical line and rectangle block. 'I think this is a depiction of a boat. The single hand above it could represent man and this triangle…' he stopped as if something important had come to him. He turned to her and she could see wonderment on his face.

'What?' she whispered.

'I think this tells the story of the ark of Deucalion, which came to rest on the slopes of Mount Parnassus.'

'So this painting isn't old enough,' Jane said sadly.

'No, no, it is. The painting style is ancient and if tested I know it will be old.'

Jane looked at him puzzled. 'But how can that be?'

Antonio looked back at her, his excitement bursting out as he said, 'It's the Oracle's painting.'

Jane stared at it. Was it possible? Could this be the sacred place of the Oracle? Could she have foreseen so far in the future to the biblical event of the Ark? Jane moved aside to let Mark and James get in to see. Her mind was in conflict. Part of it wanted to believe this was true, but another part was sceptical, cautious even.

Her light fell upon another overhang and another circle of hands. She moved over to it. In the middle of the circle was a single handprint above two pointed stone shapes. She swallowed hard. *This could be it,* she thought. She moved her light along and was shocked to see a black figure with four long legs of equal length, like table legs and on the table-top was a round head. It didn't look like a human's shape but emerging from it was a thunderbolt, which connected to a tall stick person. She moved her light along and saw the rock face had broken away. Quickly she took out her camera and found the picture of Antonio's grandfather's rock. She positioned her camera until the picture of the rock fitted the empty space on the wall. The intertwining circles with the line going through them was viewed upright. She heard a short intake of breath behind her.

'Grandfather's rock fits perfectly,' Antonio said softly. 'But what does it mean?'

James stepped forward and peered at it. 'I've seen this before but I can't remember where.' He glanced at the other figures in the painting. 'Antonio, what's this shape mean?' James was pointing to the table-like figure.

'I think it is the symbol for a higher being, the God of Thunder maybe, because of the lightning bolt.'

'We've seen that light bolt before,' James declared, glancing at Jane.

'In Africa,' she replied, looking at Mark. She saw a flash of worry reflect in his eyes. *Poor Mark,* she thought. *He finds it hard to face up to his destiny.* She took a photo of the painting and moved away to look at it. He joined her, leaving James and Antonio excitedly chatting over the meaning of the images.

'I don't think it's the same as Africa,' Mark said softly.

'Why?'

'This looks different.'

'No it doesn't. The bolt is going to a person, just like the one in Africa, and that person is you.' Jane prodded him with her finger.

'No it's not!' Mark's voice was touched with anger.

'So what does it mean?' Jane challenged.

Mark cleared his throat, 'It's going to the person we need to find.'

Jane went to speak and stopped. *Is Mark just believing now, to deflect attention from himself?* she wondered, *Or is he right?* She stared at the picture on her camera. The figure the bolt was directed at did look similar to the figure that had fallen over the rim in the African painting. 'You might be right,' she said, 'but where do we find this person?'

Mark pointed to the two intertwining circles symbol. 'Once we find out what this is, then that's where we'll find him or her.' He moved off to join the others.

Jane registered what she was feeling and surprisingly she felt he was right. She put the camera away and moved deeper into the cavern. This was too beautiful an opportunity not to explore further.

At the farthest end she found a stone with a flat surface almost like a seat and sat down. She felt tired but also a little faint. *I should have eaten more at breakfast,* she thought. All this excitement and effort to find this place had exhausted her.

She took a deep breath and recognised the same sweet scent she had smelled in her dream. Another breath and she was becoming very light-headed. Her vision began to blur and the cave around her was now fading in and out of view. At one point it was brightly lit and shadowy figures, in hooded capes, were moving in slow motion in the distance, talking to distorted people. Then they were coming towards her. She started to speak in a voice that was strange and distant and when she had finished the figures retreated quickly to the far wall. Jane shook her head to clear her vision, but the next image was of her in the cave, with red paint on her hands. She looked at them and then her eyes rolled upwards into their sockets until her sight was gone. *What is happening?* she cried in her mind for she couldn't speak. Resisting the urge to panic, she took several deep breaths and immediately found herself on the slopes of Mount Parnassus. Her hands were lifted to the heavens as if she was calling up to the gods. Around her the world was crumbling and breaking apart. Jane recognised it as her own world; the shards of black crystals pushing up through the land causing the soil to blacken and die.

A huge black thundercloud appeared above the mountain and a lightning bolt struck the top with such force that dust, ground and rock burst out, falling around her. Shielding her head with her arms she waited for the debris to disperse and when it had, there stood a beautiful woman. Long red hair curled down each side of her sculptured face, giving colour to her almost transparent skin, and then softly slipping over her delicate, pale shoulders. Bright green eyes sparkled in the grey light and a brilliant warm smile radiated from her thin lips.

Jane fell to her knees, her arms stretched out towards the woman. 'Help us,' she pleaded. Instantly, the vision was gone and instead Jane saw a beautiful garden, lush with colourful flowers, trees and life. A red stream ran through it and on the floor the symbol of the circles appeared. Jane fell bodily into the stream. It filled her nose and throat, tasting of blood. She began to choke and her body started to fray about. Somewhere in the distance she heard a man's voice shout, 'GAS! Get out of here.' She felt her body being lifted from the stream and blinking water from her eyes, she saw the red-haired woman standing in the garden calling to her. Jane couldn't hear what she was saying and the image faded the further

Jane was carried away from the stream. Jane finally lost consciousness.

'JANE, Jane!' She could hear her name being called but she couldn't see or feel anything else. The more she concentrated on the voice calling her, the more feeling came back to her body. First she got feeling in her back and torso, then her neck and head and at last she was able to open her eyes. Mark's face was above her, his eyes intently looking down at her face.

'Thank goodness,' he exclaimed. 'How are you feeling?'

Jane couldn't speak; her throat seemed to seize up every time she tried. He offered her a drink of water and supported her head as she took a sip. The touch of the bottle top on her lips felt numb, like after a visit to the dentist and she spilled some of the water down her face. Someone wiped it away with a tissue and she saw that it was James. What water went down her throat relieved the dryness and she swallowed hard.

'Wha… Wha…' her words were slurred and unformed.

'What happened?' Mark finished for her. She nodded. 'Antonio saw you collapse and realised the cavern was filling with some kind of gas.' Mark pulled her in towards him. 'I thought I had lost you!' he said kissing the top of her head.

Jane wished she could hug him, but the use of her arms was still a little while away.

'Jane, take deep breaths, it will help clear the effects of the gas,' Antonio said, his face coming into her view now. He dropped his voice to a whisper as he spoke to

Mark and James but for some reason her hearing was quite acute and she could hear what he was saying.

'If she doesn't improve in the next five minutes we need to get some help.'

Jane took deep breaths and with each one she felt herself become more responsive. After a short while she could feel her arms and legs and could speak. 'Got anything to eat, I'm starving.' The relief on the faces around her was evident. James dug into his rucksack and handed her a snack bar. Jane devoured it in seconds. He handed her another. The food was helping and she felt much better, but when she tried to get up, her legs wobbled and she sat down again. 'While we wait for my legs to come back to life, shall I tell you what I saw in the cave?' With all their attention on her, Jane relayed what had happened. After she had finished speaking there was silence. She could see Mark thinking about what she had said. James was muttering to himself, as he searched Jane's bag for something and, Antonio was just sat there grinning, his hands grasped together in front of him. He finally couldn't contain himself any longer and blurted out, 'We've found the chamber of the Oracle. It's brilliant.'

Mark turned to him sharply. 'Jane nearly died, I don't call that brilliant.'

Antonio stopped smiling and looked down to the ground, 'I'm sorry,' he murmured.

'It's okay, Antonio,' Jane said softly. 'You're right, it's a great find and it'll bring you and your grandfather some recognition.'

'But you'll need to sort out the gas first,' James quipped in. He held up a book. 'I took the liberty, my dear, to look in your bag for your guidebook, and the picture of the painting on your camera.' He opened the book and continued, 'It says that in 2001 a team, including a forensic chemist and toxicologist, discovered high concentrations of a substance called Ethylene in the waters of a spring below the temple. They reckoned that the temple of Apollo was built over a crack in the earth that emitted concentrations of hydrocarbons into the air.'

'Ethylene is a hallucinogen,' Mark said casually.

James looked up at him. 'Yes, that's what it says.'

'Does it have a sweet, fragrant smell?' Jane asked, sitting up more fully now.

James read more of the article and nodded.

'That's what's in the cave,' she stated firmly.

James put the book down and pulled up the picture of the painting on the camera. 'You see this figure with four long legs? Well I think this is the black cloud you saw in your vision. The God of Thunder, Thor. His bolt is directed to the tall figure, which maybe is the woman you saw. Perhaps she is the person we need to find.'

'In the garden of the red stream where the circles overlap,' Jane said getting to her feet. Mark grabbed her arm to steady her and she turned to him saying, 'We need to connect to the Internet. Let's get back to the hotel.'

He slipped his arm around her waist and held her tightly. 'Tomorrow.'

'But...'

'No buts,' he said cutting her off. 'You need rest and the journey back is tiring.'

Jane relaxed against his body, she was tired and her legs still struggled to support her. 'Tomorrow, then.'

***

The next day it took them longer to travel back to James's car, for despite Mark and James taking turns to carry her rucksack, Jane needed to rest frequently. At the car Jane slumped on the back seat; she was so tired. All she wanted to do was sleep.

James, Mark and Antonio were stood at the door. 'I have a signal,' James yelled after checking his mobile. 'I can connect to the Internet from here.'

In anticipation Jane sat forward, watching him tap in the description of the garden. 'Wow!' he said.

'Tell us what you're seeing?' Jane said, excited.

Mark looked over James's shoulder and said, 'You aren't going to believe this.'

'What? For goodness sake will someone tell me?' Jane moved to get out of the car, her need to know over-riding her exhaustion. James gently pushed her back and gave her the mobile. On the screen were the words "Chalice Well" and the picture was of a cover of a well, which was decorated by two overlapping circles with a bar down the centre.

'It's a well?' Jane asked, confused.

James laughed and said, 'Read on.'

She did and felt excitement flitter in her stomach. 'It… it says there is red water and it has three attributes in common with human blood: it's red, it coagulates and it's warm.' She remembered that the water she had tasted, in her vision, was like blood. *Could this be the same?*

'Where is it?' Mark asked.

Jane read more, her mind absorbing every detail. 'A

garden in Glastonbury, in England. It's believed to be linked to the christen myth that says it's the place where Joseph, of Arimathea, caught Christ's blood in a chalice.' She looked up at the three men before her, her body suddenly revived and energised. 'This is the place where we'll find our fifth person, I'm sure of it.'

CHAPTER TWELVE

Fiona opened her eyes, the ceiling above her was a dirty beige with tiny cracks creeping outwards from a centre ceiling rose. She was laid on a bed, her head nestled in a soft pillow. Gently she turned her head to the left and saw Stan sitting in a comfy cottage chair beside the bed. His smile, when he saw she was awake, highlighted his handsome, tanned face. He obviously hadn't slept for his short, hair was in disarray and the fringe, which swept over his forehead, was squashed to his skin. He leaned forward and Fiona saw a sparkle in his eyes.

'How are you feeling?' he asked.

'Better than you look,' she lied.

Stan laughed and, rubbing the stubble on his face, he said, 'You don't like the rough look?'

Fiona mused for a moment, then said, 'Suits you, but dreadful for kissing.' She laughed but quickly stopped as the pain in her chest squeezed her. She took a deep breath.

Stan got up and offered her a cup with a straw in it. He gently raised her head high enough so she could drink without choking. The water was cool and refreshing and Fiona sipped a few mouthfuls. She hadn't realised how thirsty she was, then her stomach grumbled, or how hungry.

Stan must have realised the same thing. 'I'll get you something to eat.'

'Make it a whole hog, I'm famished.'

Stan chuckled and walked way. Fiona watched him leave, noticing how his gait was like that of a cowboy. When he had gone, she took note of the room. It looked quite an old room, with walls of whitewashed stone and a door made of old plank wood, stained a dark brown. The window, opposite her bed, had a dark metal-looking frame with the glass split into nine windowpanes. The curtains looked like heavy Victorian tapestry. She looked at the wooden floor and noticed large, colourful rugs either side of the bed. Even the bed and bedside cabinets looked weathered, like they had been made from recycled wood. Through the window she saw fields spreading out into the distance.

Stan returned. 'Food's coming.'

'Where are we?'

'A small village in France, near Broon. It's a friend's house.' Stan sat down in the chair.

'France!' Fiona exclaimed. 'How did you mange that?' She stared at him shocked, remembering she hadn't got anything with her, not even her passport.

Stan smiled. 'A minor detail.'

Fiona tried to ease herself up, but the pain was too much. She groaned and rested back.

Stan got up and helped pack some pillows behind her, then he gently lifted her slowly, allowing her time, between each movement, to take deep breaths to contain her discomfort until she was sitting. He pulled out a handkerchief from his pocket and wiped away the sweat on her face. 'Do you need something for the pain?'

Fiona looked at him. 'You're a doctor too?'

Stan laughed, 'No, I've got tablets. Do you want some?'

Fiona rested back against the pillows. 'No, I think I'd prefer you to mop my brow.'

Stan shook his head in, what seemed, disbelief and returned to his chair. 'Do you realise what you've been through?' he asked.

Fiona groaned softly as she shifted herself round to get a better look at him. 'Yes,' she said, her voice trembling slightly. 'But people have died because of me and I don't know why?' She felt his eyes upon her, piercing and penetrating making her realise that she was looking at a man who had killed. She felt a shiver of anxiousness for a moment, then it was replaced by gratitude, for he had killed so she could live.

Stan's South African drawl was strong when he replied, 'Don't you feel sorry for them.'

'But the policeman,' Fiona whispered. She saw a flicker of regret in his face, before he said, 'It was unfortunate but nothing I could do.'

'Why were they after me, what did I do?' Fiona could feel tears coming to her eyes. She forced them away.

'You did nothing. They wanted Mark, or Adrian as he was known.'

Fiona looked at him, the shock of his words sinking into her mind. 'Mark isn't his real name? Does Jane know?'

Stan nodded. 'I don't have the full story, just what James has told me. The man, behind those two thugs, is called Ferrand and he wants something from Mark.'

Fiona closed her eyes, how could this be? It sounded like something from a movie and she was caught up in it. She heard him get up and felt him sit on the bed. She opened her eyes when he gently took hold of her right hand.

'You are a strong woman. What you endured, you didn't deserve.'

'But I wasn't strong enough.' The tears she had pushed back earlier returned to fill her eyes. 'I… I told them where Jane was.'

Stan stroked the palm of her hand, avoiding the two broken fingers that were strapped together. 'You survived. You did what you had to.' His hand moved to touch the swellings on her face. 'You suffered a long time, didn't you?'

Fiona nodded slightly, remembering the onslaught of punches that had hit her face. The memory triggered more tears, and desperately she tried blinking them away. Some managed to escape and trickle down her cheek onto his fingers. She saw a flash of anger ripple across his face. 'It's okay,' she whispered. 'You stopped it happening, again. You saved me.'

The anger vanished, his eyes closed and his expression seemed to be filled with pain. When he opened his eyes again, she saw a deep sadness in him. 'What happened to you?' she asked softly.

Stan turned away with a shrug and a grunt of a laugh.

'Please, I'd like to know.'

He glanced back and although he tried to smile, Fiona could see he was filled with deep emotion. 'You remind me of someone I once knew.'

'A lover maybe?' Fiona couldn't resist puckering up her swollen lips.

Stan's fading smile grew into a grin. 'I don't believe you,' he laughed.

'Believe what? I've not told you anything yet.' She heard him chuckle. 'So who was she?' Fiona pressed, sensing he was more relaxed now.

'A friend, who got into trouble and I wasn't there for her.'

'She died?' Fiona prompted softly.

He looked away and was about to get off the bed when Fiona caught hold of his hand with her thumb and forefinger. He looked back to her.

'You didn't get to her in time to save her, did you?' Fiona whispered. He nodded, dropping his gaze to the floor. 'I'm so sorry,' Fiona said gently, her fingers squeezing his hand. He remained sat on the bed, looking at the floor, in silence.

Tiredness was creeping through her body and her eyes were heavy from the holding of her tears. She didn't want to sleep but knew she couldn't fight the need of her body to rest. She relaxed her head back into the pillows and closed her eyes. 'I'm glad you saved me,' she murmured.

The mattress moved as Stan got up and, easing his hand from hers, he gently placed her hand across her body. She felt the warmth of his breath near her face and heard him whisper, 'I'm glad I saved you too.' Then his lips gently touched her swollen cheek for a second, before he moved away. As she drifted off to sleep, she had one thought: *I hope he's still single.*

★★★

Fiona was sat up in bed just finishing eating a bowl of warm, nourishing porridge. Her strength was returning and the pain in her chest and stomach was easing every day. She wasn't sure how long it had been since Stan had got her out of the hospital, but she calculated that three days had gone by since she had first woken up in the room. A local French doctor had visited her everyday and whilst she didn't understand what he was saying, she got the idea that he was pleased with her progress.

She hadn't seen much of Stan, although she knew he often sat with her at night when she was sleeping. She had caught a glimpse of him one night, when the pain had woken her, unexpectedly.

There was a faint knock on the door and a small, slim, dark-haired woman entered.

'*Bonjour*, Fiona.'

'*Bonjour*, Madame Herbert.'

The woman tutted but smiled, 'Emilie, it be Emilie. *Tu* friend.'

Fiona smiled at Emilie's broken English. She thought Emilie looked over fifty years old, with grey streaks in her ebony-coloured hair and crow-feet wrinkles at the corner of her eyes. She leaned back and let Emilie take the tray.

'Food good?' Emilie asked, looking at her.

'Excellent,' Fiona replied, rubbing her stomach.

Emilie nodded. 'You well soon.' She turned and left the room, passing Stan in the doorway.

Fiona was pleased to see him again. She had been worried that their last conversation had put him off speaking with her. Today, however, he had shaved and looked even more handsome than before. She nodded admiringly at him. 'My, you spruce up well.'

He frowned and then nodded when Fiona stroked her own chin. 'And you are recovering quickly,' he replied, sitting in the chair.

'So what's new? Have you heard from Jane?'

'I've had a text from James. They are on their way to Glastonbury.'

Stan explained to her what Jane and Mark were searching for. She still found it hard to believe it was happening. Jane was her boss but also her friend and she knew that if Jane was doing this, it must be important. 'Are you going to meet them?'

'No. I'm here to protect you.'

Fiona felt a shiver of fear return. 'Do you think they'll try again?'

'No.' The bluntness of his reply puzzled her.

'What's the point of you being here, then?'

His penetrating stare was making her feel slightly uncomfortable, so she quickly said, 'I know I'm charming and a good catch…' she paused to brush a strand of hair away from her face. '…when I'm looking my best that is. And who wouldn't want to stay in my company, all the time, but if you give me a quick kiss…' she blew a kiss at him, '…it will break the spell and you'll be able to leave.' She squinted a quick look at him and saw the smile start, then she started to giggle herself. 'That's better, such a stern look you have.'

'Focus is what it's called,' Stan replied.

'Well, not the kind of focus I like,' Fiona retorted.

'Anyway back to my question, why can't you just leave me here. It's safe isn't it?'

Stan leant forward so his elbows were resting on his knees and his hands clasped together under his chin. 'Yes it's safe, for now, but I won't risk it.'

'Why?'

'Because of what happened last time.'

Fiona felt the chill return. 'What happened?'

Stan waved her question away, as a way of dismissing it.

'Stan, don't give me a puzzle and leave me wondering about the answer. There could be something important for me to know.' She could see he was hesitating but also thinking about what she had said. 'Please tell me what happened.'

He cleared his throat and Fiona could see he was finding it difficult to start. 'It's to do with that other woman, isn't it? The one you couldn't save.'

Stan just gazed at the floor and when he spoke his voice was quiet. 'I was protecting her from her rich boyfriend, a nasty, brutal man. It was after I had left the army and I was working as a bodyguard.' He swallowed and looked up. 'Extracting her from the boyfriend's lair went easily. The thugs he had guarding her were no match for me.'

Fiona could believe that.

He continued, 'I took her to a safe place and she stayed with some people I knew.'

Like you did for me, Fiona thought.

Stan stood up and paced the room as he spoke. 'I'd known her from childhood, she was called Stacy and it was her parents who hired me. After a week of hiding, she persuaded me that she was safe and it was okay to leave her. I knew I couldn't stay with her forever and I had to do other work, but I also knew what kind of person her boyfriend was and he didn't like to lose.'

'So you left her?' Fiona cut in.

'Yes, but with restrictions. They were to safe guard her and the people she was with.'

'What happened?' Fiona whispered.

'She called her parents.'

Fiona looked at him puzzled, 'So?'

Stan stopped pacing and turned to her. 'She told them where she was.'

Fiona shrugged, thinking, *how could that be a problem?*

Stan's voice was hard and cold. 'Her parents had a visit from the boyfriend and his men.'

Fiona felt her stomach sink. She began to comprehend what had happened next. 'He... he tortured them?' she stammered.

Stan shook his head, 'No, only threatened to. Then, when he got the information, he killed them.'

Fiona's eyes widened. 'And what about your friends she was staying with?'

Stan's hands clenched into fists, 'He killed them too.'

Fiona felt a nervousness creep through her body as she asked, 'And Stacy?'

Stan stared at her but it was as if he was looking elsewhere. 'The boyfriend beat her first, then cut her face to bits, before cutting out her heart.'

Fiona swallowed the lump that had appeared in her throat. 'How do you know this?' she croaked.

Stan's eyes narrowed, his face emotionless. 'Because I got there an hour after it happened and he had left me a message in her blood.'

'What was it?' Fiona whispered, hardly able to speak.

'Stan's voice held no emotion, 'I will kill you.'

'What did you do?'

Stan moved towards the door.

'What did you do?' Fiona called after him.

His hand rested on the door latch, then he turned, his face rigid, his lips tight together. When he spoke the tone of his voice was like ice, 'I killed him and all his family.'

For a moment Fiona saw the beast hidden in the face; the killer with no remorse, then he turned away and left the room.

She rested back on the pillows and took a deep breath. Stan was a man of extremes all right, but even though she had seen his deadly side, she also knew in her heart that he was good. He both scared and excited her. 'Remind myself not to push for an answer next time,' she told herself. But at least now she knew what message the story had for her. "Be careful what you do." Phew! She wouldn't forget that story anytime soon. But it had raised a concern in her… what about her own parents?

CHAPTER THIRTEEN

Jane's excitement was building as they approached Glastonbury. The trip from Greece had taken several days with each of them taking turns to drive. The road brought them to the bottom of the high street, along Magdalene Street. On the right side, Jane saw the grand entrance to Glastonbury Abbey and on the left side there were a few shop windows and houses that looked like they offered guest rooms. She saw people strolling along the pavement and had to look twice when, amongst them, she saw someone dressed as an elf and a fairy. 'Did you see that?' she exclaimed.

James slowed down so he could see better. 'Weird lot down here,' he muttered to himself.

'Why do you say that?' she challenged.

'Well, look at them. They must be so far from reality to dress like that.'

'Maybe they want to wear what they like and not be judged on their decisions,' she countered, watching the people walking along the street. No one was staring at them or making whispering comments, they were being accepted as they were and it looked really natural.

They followed the road round to the right, passing a monument. More shops selling crystals and medieval clothes lined each side of the single street. Half way up there was a seating area and Jane saw men dressed in ragged clothes drinking from beer cans. 'They certainly have a variety of people here,' she said.

Mark turned to her. 'I've been reading about this place and they say that Glastonbury accepts anyone and everyone. You have really spiritual people here and you have those that may have lost their way.' He indicated to the people Jane had seen.

'There are all sorts of belief systems here too, from Pagan, Witchcraft, Buddhism to Catholic and Christianity. This place seems to be the only area where they all can be together without conflict. And look here.' He pointed to a picture in the book of a king. 'The myth of King Arthur, and also there's stories from the Christian beliefs, concerning Jesus and Mary Magdalene.'

'This place is amazing,' Jane mused as she spotted a little girl walking with her mother, both dressed in fairy outfits.

At the top of the road they turned right and carried on until they got to Chilkwell Street, where Jane spotted the entrance to the Chalice Well . 'There, there!' she yelled pointing to the left. James drove in and Jane was out of the car before it had hardly stopped. When James and Mark joined her, she paid the entrance fee and entered the garden. The narrow pathway led them through the beautifully laid out garden, where, every so often, there was a place to sit and saviour the quiet, serene atmosphere.

Just off to the right, a set of steps led them down to an open area, to a large red pool that was being filled by water flowing down through seven bowls. Swirling eddies of water fell into the pool, which was shaped as two overlapping circles. Jane looked at the leaflet she had been given at the entrance. 'The pool is called the Vesica Pool. It has the shape we're looking for, but it's not the well.' She pointed towards two large trees, which seemed to form a gateway or entrance to the rest of the garden. 'This way I think.'

They walked up the grass, past a thorny tree and through the two larger trees. Jane had an overwhelming feeling of being welcomed and that she knew this place. It was as if the trees were old friends and she wanted to give them a hug. She controlled the urge, knowing James and Mark would probably want to move on. Instead she just gently touched each of them in turn, feeling a warmth in the palm of her hand that seemed to travel to her heart, making her feel wonderfully calm and reflective.

She saw Mark wave to her to come on, so reluctantly she whispered goodbye and caught up with him. The path took them further into the garden, to an oblong pool of the red water, being fed by a small fountain at the far end. The sign said it was a healing pool and indicated you could walk through the water. Jane hesitated, tempted to try it out, but the others had moved on, so she followed them. They reached an area where a lion's head was pouring water into a glass. Jane couldn't resist; she filled the glass. The water had a rusty colour to it so she carefully took a sip. It tasted like blood. She handed it to Mark who screwed up his face.

'Try it. It tastes of blood.'

Mark took a sip and reluctantly swallowed it. He passed the glass to James, who looked at it closely. 'Hmm, the colour must come from the red iron in the water.' He took a sip. 'And it has an unusual taste that could be mistaken for blood.' He put the glass back. 'I can understand why people think this is where the blood of Christ was buried.'

'Wouldn't you if you didn't know the science?' Jane asked.

James nodded. 'Yes, science can explain most things but not everything.'

They moved on and just to the right Jane saw the well. It was in a circular stone area, with the well lid raised. The symbol on the lid was exactly what Jane had seen. She sat on the small wall surrounding the well and read the leaflet. 'It says this symbol is called the Vesica Piscis. It's an ancient symbol that symbolises the union of heaven and earth or spirit and matter.'

Mark sat next to her. 'And you think this is where you'll find the woman to help us?'

Jane nodded and scanned the quiet, empty area around them. 'We'll wait a bit,' she said hopefully.

'I've been looking at the symbol and I think I understand its meaning.' Mark took the leaflet from her and followed the top circle with his finger. 'The heaven or spirit.' Then he did the same with the bottom circle. 'The earth or matter.' He followed the line that went through them. 'The lance holds them together and here,' he pointed to the oval centre, 'is where they combine, heaven and earth, matter and spirit become one. A power spot.'

Jane frowned, 'So?'

Mark laughed, 'I'm not sure yet, don't know why that suddenly came to me.'

She took his hand and squeezed it. 'Thank you for coming with me. I'm glad you're here.'

'Hmm, not sure it was the right decision though. I still feel I should be at the lab.' He gave a big sigh, then said, 'I hope you won't be too disappointed, Jane, if she doesn't exist.'

Jane smiled. 'She does and in this place, I just feel it will happen.' She kissed him gently on the lips.

James stopped examining the well and stood up. 'I think I'll leave you two to it,' he said, stepping out of the area and disappearing up the path.

After half an hour of sitting and staring at the well, Mark got up. 'I'm going to find James, do you want to come?'

Jane shook her head. 'I want to stay here… in case she comes.' She saw him nod his head and step out of the well area.

After a while, she got up and rubbed her bottom, the coldness of the stone seat had numbed it. When the feeling came back, she knelt down by the well head, peering into the dark, still water, watching her reflection. The water suddenly shivered in ripples and she looked up, wondering what had caused the vibration, but there was no one there. She glanced back, the water had stilled again and she let herself be drawn into her reflection. Her eyes softly focused on her face and she saw it transform into a wrinkly, hooded old woman, who was smiling at her. It flickered slightly and her face became much younger, with smooth skin and alert eyes. She stared further into the image, and her face turned into a landscape, quite barren, with mountains high on each side of a ravine. It looked stunning, but also ominous as the blackness of the water was creeping into the edge of the image, gently swallowing it until nothing was left but the still, black well water. Jane shivered and returned to her seat. Was that a premonition or just her mind playing tricks? She dearly hoped it was just her mind.

Hours went by and Jane kept on shifting her seat and standing up to walk round the well. She had not allowed herself to look into the well again and had occupied her mind with visions of how everything would be okay; of thoughts of what would happen between her and Mark, when this was over. Did he still love her as much as he had when they were in Jersey? Did she still love him as deeply, now all this had happened to her? She certainly hadn't expected to be so involved in escaping Ferrand, but neither had Mark expected to be found.

She laughed at herself for still recognising and calling him Mark, and not his real name, Adrian. But she could never see him as Adrian for she had fallen in love with the man she knew as Mark. She caught a glimpse of him and James walking past on the path. They looked in but didn't stop this time, as they had done several times before. Instead they moved to sit on a bench just outside the well area, talking quietly together. She wondered if they were talking about her and whether they thought she had gone nuts. Either way she didn't care, but she was thankful they had not abandoned her.

As the afternoon drew late, Mark stepped into the well area. 'We need to find a place to stay. We can come back tomorrow.'

'It's not closing time yet,' Jane said urgently, wanting to be available every minute she could.

He took her arm and pulled her to her feet. 'You want this too much. It's time to let it go. Remember the cave in Greece?'

Jane sighed deeply and holding back the disappointment, she said, 'Okay, you're right.'

James joined them and they made their way back along the path, past an area on the right where a figure of an angel overlooked a seat. Jane just caught a glimpse of someone sat there, wearing a long medieval-type dress and a scarf over her head. As they reached the steps to the oblong healing pool, Jane looked back. The woman was walking up to the well area and just before she entered the stone circle around it, she pulled off her head scarf. To Jane's astonishment, long red hair fell down her back.

Jane stopped abruptly and grabbed Mark's arm. 'It's her, it's her.'

Mark looked in the same direction as Jane.

'That woman has been sitting at the angel seat for at least an hour,' James said looking between them. 'I thought it weird at the time but,' he looked at Jane, 'not as weird as you sitting at the well for all that long.'

Jane ignored his sarcastic comment and quickly walked back to the well area. The woman was sitting quietly, her long red hair seemed to shine like it had stardust in it and her petite frame looked exquisite in the dark-green medieval dress. The woman looked up and surprise registered on her pale, almost sculptured face.

'I… I'm sorry to disturb you,' Jane stuttered. 'But I was wondering if I could talk to you?'

The woman nodded gracefully and indicated for Jane to sit beside her. As Jane took her seat, Mark and James came to the steps.

'They are with me. Do you mind if they join us?'

Again the woman just shook her head, but didn't say anything.

Jane cleared her throat, 'This may sound strange but we are looking for someone who will help us and we have followed signs that have led us here.' Jane pointed to the well head and paused, looking for a reaction, but the woman just looked at her with sparkling, soft, bright green eyes.

'I had a vision of this person and she looks exactly like you. I know you may think I'm mad, but…' Jane stopped, thinking that perhaps she was mad and making a fool of herself.

'I do not think you mad.' The woman said in a voice that was angelic. 'I have been waiting every day at this well for a sign or message, and now you have come.'

'You have?' Jane gave a nervous laugh of relief, 'I can't believe it.'

'I had a dream and was told by the god, Apollo, to come here and wait.' She diverted her eyes to the well and her pale lips parted in a timid smile.

Jane looked at Mark and James, but they were looking at the woman as if captivated by her delicate beauty.

James suddenly stirred, 'My dearest Lady of Avalon, may we explain ourselves to you and tell you our story?' His words seemed to flow seamlessly from his lips.

The woman smiled warmly and for a moment she glanced up to him before diverting her eyes towards Jane. 'The gardens are closing soon. Please come to my home and have some tea with me.' She looked back to James, 'You can then tell me your story.'

Jane watched as a huge blush hit James's face. He

took out a handkerchief and pretended to blow his nose.

The woman rose and Jane followed her onto the path back to the entrance, with Mark and James following behind. In the car park Jane saw only their own vehicle and realised the woman must have walked. James opened the passenger front door for her and she slipped in. They drove back along Chilkwell Street towards the top of the high street. Just past a walled entrance to a large house, surrounded by beautiful gardens, the woman directed them to turn left. The road narrowed and she pointed to a rough track to the right. James gently eased the car onto the track and pulled up alongside a small terraced house half way down, on the left. He quickly got out and ran round to open the door for her. The woman eased herself off the front seat and gently took the supportive hand James offered her.

Jane watched, smiling. James seemed to have allowed his gentleman's up bringing to fully envelope him and the way the woman moved and acted, she could see why.

The woman opened the house door and beckoned them to enter. James went first. The house was tiny. The entrance hall barely big enough for two, so Jane had to wait until James moved into the room on the left, before she could enter. She followed him in and saw they were in a small lounge. A two-seated, old, Victorian-style sofa was against the wall behind the open door. In front of it was a hearth with an open fire that was lit and burning gently behind a mesh protector. Either side of the fire there stood huge Geodes of a purple crystal, sparkling and shining as if they had recently been polished. On the mantelpiece there were two old iron-cast candlestick holders, which the woman was lighting; and more clear crystal points, four or five inches high from base to point.

'Please sit,' the woman said, gesturing to the sofa, whilst sitting down on a single wooden chair next to the fire.

Before Jane decided to squeeze herself between Mark and James, she said, 'I'm afraid we've been extremely rude. My name is Jane; this is Mark and James.'

The woman smiled and extended her pale hand to Jane. 'I am pleased to meet you. My name is Theola, but I like to be called Lola.'

Jane shook her hand, noticing that whilst it first felt delicate to the touch, like a piece of porcelain, once they shook the grip was subtly strong.

'Lola, a beautiful name, my dear,' James cooed, 'does it have any special meaning?'

Lola diverted her eyes to the floor; she said with a smile, 'I've been told Theola means "Gift from God".'

Jane nearly stumbled as she sat down. 'A gift from God is exactly what that painting in the cave symbolised,' she whispered to Mark. 'How did you get given this name, if you don't mind me asking?' Jane asked, getting herself comfortable.

Lola looked up. 'It was the nurses at the hospital. You see I was found abandoned on the hospital steps when I was a day old, on 29th of February, in one of the worst winters they have ever had. So because I survived, they decided to call me Theola.'

'And you never knew your parents?' Jane probed, intrigued on how this woman's very existence could have been predicted so long ago.

'No, there was no trace of them and they never came forward to the police requests in the paper.'

'Jane, have you no feelings?' James scolded, looking upset.

Lola's voice was like soft music, it flowed effortlessly and its tones were gentle and sweet. 'It's perfectly okay, please don't be sad for me. I only have love for them. They gave me to the world and I'm so very pleased to be here.'

How could someone be like that? Jane thought.

Lola got up, her movement seamlessly smooth. 'I shall get some tea for you and you can tell me why you're here.' Jane detected a slight touch of excitement in her voice.

Whilst drinking the tea and eating homemade biscuits, James told Lola everything; from the black crystals appearing, to finding the painting at the Oracle cave in Greece. All the time Jane watched Lola as she listened, registering only one emotion in Lola's face, one of sadness when she learned the crystals were dying.

James leaned back into the sofa and drank the last drops of his tea. The room was silent. Lola was very still, her eyes fixed on the two large purple crystals on the floor. 'The crystals are dying?' she whispered to no one in particular. Jane was sure she saw the glow from the crystals dampen slightly, but she couldn't be sure. Then Lola turned to look at them. 'So you think I am this fifth person in the painting?'

Jane nodded.

Lola immediately smiled and shot out her hand towards Jane. 'I want to show you something.'

Jane got up and took Lola's hand, allowing herself to be led out of the room and up the stairs to the bedroom. When Lola put on the light, Jane gasped in amazement. 'Unbelievable,' she whispered. There was one double bed in the middle of the room against the back wall and in every other vacant space there were crystals of all colours and shapes. They shone out such a brilliant light that it was almost too strong to gaze at them.

'They are my friends and I love them,' Lola said, smiling.

Jane turned to her and grabbed both her hands in excitement. 'It is you! Oh, Lola, you are going to save us.'

Lola smiled even more and in response the crystals seemed to shine brighter. Jane waved to Mark and James to come to her and they came up the stairs. 'Take a look at this, Mark, and tell me I'm wrong.'

Mark stood in the doorway, his eyes went to Lola who was sitting on the bed gently cradling some clusters of sparkling, creamy crystals. He turned to Jane and she could see lightness in his eyes and wonderment in his smile. 'It feels… indescribably lovely,' he said softly. He blinked and the lightness was gone. 'I need to do some tests.'

Jane frowned. 'Why do you always break the moment?' He looked puzzled. 'You know, putting your scientific mind into gear.' He just shrugged and gave her a hug. 'We've done it, we've found her,' she whispered in his ear.

James eased himself past them and stood just inside the doorway. Jane could see his eyes were focused on Lola and his whole face beamed.

‘Amazing,’ he whispered.

Mark eased away from Jane and turned to him, saying, ‘We need to find a place to stay for the night, James.’

‘Amazing,’ was all James said.

Mark placed a hand on his shoulder. ‘A place to sleep?’ he repeated.

‘Amazing,’ James said again, in a far away voice.

Lola joined him at the door and he gently moved aside for her. ‘I know the lady at the Abbey House, just up the road. I’ll ask if she has any rooms for you.’ She slipped down the stairs to the phone and James followed her.

‘Well, I think we’ve cracked it,’ Jane said excitedly, rubbing her hands together. She saw Mark’s serious look and stopped. ‘What?’

‘We have to do some tests to be sure.’

‘Oh you stick in the mud. Lighten up. You can see the effect she has on the crystals. It’ll be fine.’ She grabbed his arm and together they went down stairs.

CHAPTER FOURTEEN

Abbey House was a beautiful old building with stone outer walls and the smell of old polished wood inside. Jane and Mark shared a room that was quite basic, but comfortable. It had a double bed, wooden wardrobe, a sink in the corner, and a chair and desk.

It was early morning and Jane stretched as she sat on the edge of the bed. Her sleep had been dreamless and she felt refreshed. She slipped on her dressing gown and left the room to go to the bathroom just down the corridor. The old house had a great feel about it and she could just imagine walking this corridor at night with a candle, like they did in the old days. Thankfully the house had been upgraded to electric bulb.

On returning to the room she noticed a stream of light coming through a gap in the heavy-set curtains. She opened them slightly so as not to disturb Mark and looked out of the window. Their room overlooked the lush green lawn, heavily laden with dew, and the grounds that led to the abbey ruins. Dawn was coming and the old broken stone walls of the abbey looked majestic against the lightening sky. Even in its ruined state, Jane got a sense of how powerful the abbey building must have been in its time. It was now a tourist attraction and the place where King Arthur was supposed to be buried.

She heard a groan from the bed. 'Is it morning already?'

'Yes, sleepy head.' She moved to the wardrobe and

dressed in walking trousers, a t-shirt and thick jumper. From looking outside it would seem the temperature had dropped. She turned to Mark as he got out of bed. 'You best get ready, we're meeting James downstairs at 8.30.'

They found James in the large foyer, pacing up and down. He greeted them and then quickly moved to the front door.

'What's the rush?' Jane asked as he opened the door for her.

'Rush? Not rushing, just hungry that's all.'

Jane smiled as she made her way down the stone steps onto the gravel path. Hungry? Perhaps it had more to do with the fact they had arranged to meet Lola for breakfast at the Hungry Monkey on the high street.

The air had a chill to it and the sun was shining between batches of grey cloud. They walked, at quite a quick pace, to the entrance and turned left to reach the high street. Ten minutes later they were at the cafe and James hurried to where Lola was sitting. 'Beautiful morning, my dear,' he said.

Lola smiled shyly, her hands around a steaming cup of what looked like hot water with a slice of lemon.

Jane sat next to her, noticing she was wearing a cream flowery dress with a large pink crystal in the shape of a heart around her neck.

'Did you sleep well?' Lola asked her.

'Yes, the Abbey House is so peaceful and quiet. And you?'

Lola smiled in a little more relaxed way. 'I had a dream I wish to tell you about. But please order your breakfast first.'

Jane nodded and after looking at the menu she settled for porridge with fruit and a cup of herbal tea. She noticed Mark and James were struggling to choose and then realised the cafe was vegetarian. They both settled for cereal and coffee.

'Tell us of your dream my dear, Lola,' James coaxed her.

'Let me explain that my dreams usually have a message and I think from what you told me yesterday, you would be interested in this.'

'Of course, of course,' James cut in.

Lola gently rested her hands in her lap and said, 'My goddess guide, Brighid, came to me. She is the Goddess of Fire and Water. She took me into the past, to the time before the flood. I saw how we had become greedy, uncaring and spiteful to each other.' She took a little breath, as if remembering this had caused her pain. 'I saw a man and heard a voice tell him to build a boat that would withstand a mighty flood. Brighid told me that the spirit of the waters rose up and wiped away the badness. Those on the boat were saved and it came to rest on a mountain.'

'That's the biblical story of the flood,' Mark said. 'But what has this to do with us now?'

'Brighid told me that the true purpose of the flood was to save us and the Earth.' Lola paused and took something from her small material bag. It was a clear crystal. 'The crystals hold the balance within everything. Their vibration can be programmed for good or bad.'

Mark nodded. 'I know that, but the connection?'

Lola smiled sweetly at the crystal and it seemed to shine

brighter. 'Before the flood, man's negative thoughts had began to influence the crystals, creating negative vibrations that were spreading throughout the Earth.' She paused.

'Of course, of course,' James said, excitedly. 'The flood wiped out those people creating the bad vibes only leaving those whose thoughts were loving and pure,' he smiled at her.

Lola's eyes focused on him for a brief second and she nodded. 'The crystals changed and our Earth and us, were saved.'

The waitress came with their breakfasts and when she had gone, Jane said, 'So are you saying that we're going to have another flood?'

'No!' Mark cut in sharply. Jane turned to him as he continued, 'We have…' he stopped, then said, 'I have created something that is self-generating. Even if everyone on the earth was wiped out, the crystals would continue to destroy themselves.'

Jane heard a slight whimper come from Lola and when she looked at her, she saw sadness in her face. The crystal in her hand had dropped in brightness too.

'But if good people just energise good thoughts into the crystals, wouldn't it stop it?' Jane persisted, not wanting to believe that there was nothing that could be done.

'Good people have negative thoughts too, but that's not the problem. The virus is self-sustaining.' Mark dropped his head, as if in shame.

'But, there must be some hope!' Jane cried.

Lola gently touched her hand and Jane felt gentle energy flowing into it.

'There is hope, Jane. Brighid told me a saviour had been created. Someone who can change the crystals' vibrations.'

'Is that you?' Jane asked.

Lola smiled warmly. 'She didn't say, but I think so. Ever since I can remember, I have loved crystals and they respond to me as you can see,' she paused and looked at the crystal, which brightened. 'If I can be of help, I would like that very much.'

Jane gripped Lola's hand and squeezed it. She felt an overwhelming feeling of compassion fill her. 'You are our angel!' she said softly. She turned to Mark in time to see his face suddenly take on an anxious look. Making eye contact with him, she saw his slight head nod to the cafe door. 'Well. I think I need to walk off my breakfast. Mark, fancy a walk down the high street?' Mark nodded.

'I'll stay with Lola and sort out our travel arrangements then,' James blurted out.

'Travel?' Lola asked.

'Yes, my dear, to Africa. How are you fixed?'

Lola's face brightened and Jane saw it was almost shining in radiance.

'Africa, birth place of humanity. That'll be so wonderful,' she said gleefully.

Jane got up with Mark. 'We'll see you later then. Where shall we meet you, James?'

'Oh please come to my home,' Lola said, her eyes bright like an excited child. 'I want to hear more of Africa from James.'

Jane saw the look of complete satisfaction on James's face and she grinned. 'We'll see you at Lola's house then.'

She took Mark's arm and they left the cafe. Outside she squeezed his arm. 'What's wrong?'

He gave a big sigh. 'Lola isn't going to be able to save the crystals.'

'Why?' Jane was shocked.

'Because it has got too big.'

'But… but if Lola can change the vibration of the large crystal in Ferrand's mine, it will change the rest, surely?'

Mark took her hand from his arm and held it. They began to walk down the street. 'Until I try her with some infected crystals, I don't know.'

'Try her? You don't mean she has to touch them, do you?'

Mark nodded.

'But she could be infected like James's men were.'

'How else do you think she would do it?' Mark said stiffly.

Jane felt her joy slowly slip away. 'Could she not think it?' she said flippantly.

Mark pulled her to a stop. 'No! So before you get your expectations up, I think you need to consider the dangers to Lola. I expect she will have to make contact with the main transmitting crystal and I don't know if Lola has enough goodness in her to repel the negative vibes being sent through it.' He looked away as if thinking of something else.

'What else?' Jane said annoyed.

He turned back. 'The picture in Africa showed me using the universal power.'

'Yes, of course. It will help Lola send her goodness

into the crystal. That's the answer.' Jane felt her spirit rise, but the disbelieving look on Mark's face pulled her up.

'I don't know if it will do that, but it could…' he stopped.

'It could what?'

'Kill her.'

Jane felt as if Mark had punched every hope from her body. Every positive thought demolished in just those two words.

'You see, I can bring the energy into being, but it's unpredictable and very powerful. When I did it last time, it nearly consumed me, so I put it into something else. It consumed that and everything around it.'

Jane gulped, 'I… I didn't know.' She felt lost and completely helpless.

Mark pulled her hand into the crook of his arm and walked on. 'I need to do some work on this. There may be a way of creating a master crystal.' He patted her hand. 'Don't despair, Jane. I'll try to find away to do this without hurting Lola.'

Jane looked up into his face and he smiled, but the look in his eyes gave her no hope he could do what he said. Jane let her head drop and tried to distract herself by looking into a shop window selling crystals. The pieces in the window twinkled back at her like stars in the night sky, but their pleasant colours couldn't penetrate the deep gloom that was slowly crushing her from inside.

* * *

An hour later they were back at Lola's house. Lola answered the door. Her smile was stunning and the warm glow on her face showed how happy she was. Jane could not remember seeing anyone who could radiate such warm, loving energy as Lola was doing now. It connected with her own aura and lifted her mood.

'You had a lovely walk?' Lola asked as Jane and Mark entered the house.

'Yes,' Jane replied softly, before taking a seat on the wooden chair by the fire in the lounge. James was on the sofa, smiling. She hadn't ever seen him so happy.

'Trip is all booked, we leave tomorrow,' he said eagerly.

Mark moved across the tiny room to stand behind Jane, whilst Lola returned to her seat next to James. They smiled at each other and James took hold of Lola's hand. It was a wonderful sight, but Jane couldn't rejoice in seeing it. She and Mark had decided to tell Lola the risks involved and she knew James wasn't going to like it. She saw James look over to her.

'Well you two don't look overly pleased, what's up?'

Jane glanced at Mark and he cleared his throat with a cough. 'James, I've been thinking about how we are going to reverse the effects of the crystals.'

'That's good,' James said, distracted with pushing back Lola's hair from her face and kissing her cheek. Lola smiled shyly and looked to the floor.

'Ah… well… I think, but I can't be sure that…' Mark paused struggling with the words.

James laughed, 'Spit it out man, for goodness' sake.'

'There's a risk to Lola.'

James stopped laughing, his head swung round sharply and he stared at Mark, 'What risk?'

Mark pulled at his jumper neckline and placed his

other hand on the back of Jane's chair for support. Jane put her hand over his and gave it a squeeze.

'What risk?' James repeated.

'She will need to touch the infected crystals.'

'NO. NO WAY!' James shouted, rising from the sofa.

Mark squared up to him, 'What did you expect, James. That, having found our fifth person, everything was going to be okay?'

James pointed accusingly at Mark, 'This… this is all your fault. You got us into this mess so you can fucking get us out of it.'

'I can't without Lola's help.'

'Help! You're going to kill her!'

'It's the only way.'

James shook his head violently. 'NO! You find another way. I won't let you do this.'

Jane saw anger on Mark's face. She stood up fearing there would be a fight.

'You hypocrite! I bet you wouldn't be saying this if Lola had been a man!'

James went for Mark and Mark shoved him hard in the chest forcing him to step backwards. Jane slipped in between them and was about to shout, when Lola suddenly leapt up screaming. 'STOP IT, stop it!'

James quickly turned round as she took hold of his arm and Jane could see tears streaming down her pale face. 'Please don't fight. I don't like these feelings,' she sobbed.

Jane noticed a sudden gloom in the room and a feeling of sadness filled her. Mark stood back and Jane felt him take her hand.

James immediately pulled Lola to him and hugged her. 'Don't cry, my dear, it's okay.' Lola held him tightly and gradually the atmosphere in the room lightened. 'I won't let anything happen to you, I promise,' he said, wiping away her tears.

She touched his face. 'I know, but you cannot control my destiny. I have been waiting for my time to come and this is it.'

James shook his head, but she stopped him with her hands cupping his face. She kissed him tenderly on the lips.

Jane felt a lump appear in her throat and swallowed it quickly.

Lola made James sit back on the sofa and she snuggled next to him. 'Please tell me the risks, Mark.'

Jane sat down on the chair and listened as Mark told Lola what he had told her. She saw James flinch and stiffen with anger, but Lola just placed her hand on his chest and the emotions disappeared. Jane wished Lola would take away the heaviness that seemed to be permanently on her own shoulders.

After Mark had finished speaking there was silence and then Lola said, 'I understand what you are saying. I want to help.'

'No, Lola, please,' James pleaded

Lola put her finger to his lips, 'Is it not true that if I don't try, I will still die once the virus reaches here?'

James's eyes closed for a second and when they opened, Jane saw they were watery.

'But if I do help, there may be a chance that we can save every one and free my crystal friends from this virus.' She turned to Jane and Mark. 'Tomorrow we leave at 7am. If it pleases James, I would like him to stay here tonight.'

Jane saw him nod slightly and then rest his head on Lola's shoulder. All the pleasure she had seen in him when they arrived was gone and she felt awful because it was all her fault.

CHAPTER FIFTEEN

It was past midnight and Fiona slipped out of the bed as gently as she could. She had memorised the exact layout of the room so that she could leave the light off. The thin nightgown Emilie had given her clung to her body, where the patches of sweat were still wet from the exertion of getting up. She moved slow and tenderly to the door, and willing it to be quiet, she lifted the latch. There was a slight creak, making her freeze for a moment. She listened. The house was quiet.

Fiona moved out of the room into a small corridor. Its tiled floor was cold to her bare feet. With her eyes adjusting to the darkness, she could see the house layout. She remembered that everything was on one floor and that the bathroom was right next to her room on the left. She moved past it, stepping silently so she didn't wake anyone.

Behind the first door, after the bathroom, she heard a man snoring. It was either Emilie's husband, or Stan. Somehow she didn't think Stan would snore. The next room was silent. She didn't know if Stan was in there but she took extra care not to make a noise as she tiptoed past into the kitchen. Just after lunch, she had scouted the house out, when she surprised Emilie by taking her soup bowl back to the kitchen. It had been worth the effort as she discovered the kitchen was the only room that had a telephone.

Since her talk with Stan in the morning, she had worried about her parents and her friend, Caroline with her husband and children. They would know what had happened at the hospital and would be worried about her. More importantly, what if what happened to her, happened to them. She wouldn't be able to live with herself if any of them got hurt. She needed them to be safe. She needed to warn them.

Emilie had told her, at lunchtime, that Stan had gone out shortly after he and Fiona had chatted. That was hours ago and he hadn't returned by the time they had all gone to bed.

Fiona was desperate to contact her family and Caroline. It would only be a short phone call; a quick word to tell them to go somewhere safe and she wouldn't tell them where she was. The memory of what happened to Stacy was still vivid in her mind.

She paused in the kitchen doorway to rest. The telephone was hung on the wall by the back door at the far end. She moved across the floor, picked it up and listened. The ready-to-dial tone was clear and she tapped in the number for her parents. The phone clicked with each press. Then she heard it try to make a connection. The unobtainable tone came back to her.

A feeling of panic began to build in her stomach and she tried again. When she was half way through tapping in the number, she remembered she was in France. *The international code, idiot*, she thought to herself. Quickly she cleared the number and began to input it again.

'Do you really want to get killed?' Stan's voice came from behind her.

Fiona jumped and dropped the phone; the last few numbers un-entered.

She turned round slowly. Most of his body was in shadow, except his face and the shiny barrel of a handgun.

'I… I was worried about my parents and…' She didn't finish her sentence. The penetrating look he was giving her made her heart pound in fear. She tentatively bent down to retrieve the phone, her eyes still on him.

Stan's movement was so quick. He was upon her before she realised it, pushing her body back against the wall. His gun arm across her chest. Fiona caught her breath at the pain and the force he was exerting on her body.

'And what about Emilie and Andre, would you risk their lives too, after what they have done for you!'

Fiona saw the spittle on his lips and the glare of anger in his eyes.

First, she felt like crying, the guilt at what he was suggesting she'd done rising within her. Then came anger. How dare he stop her. She had a right to safe guard her parents. Stacy had made the mistake, not her! She brought up one of her legs and kneed him in his lower area, whilst simultaneously using the heal of her right hand on his chest to push him as hard as she could. Her unexpected action had surprised him, but only for a second before his arm forced her back harder into the wall.

His rough treatment of her brought up the rage she had subconsciously suppressed of being violated by the PI and his gorilla, and being helpless to do anything. In desperation she went for him. 'I hate you, I hate you!' she yelled, flailing at his face with her hands, and kicking out with her legs. Stan took everything she gave him until he suddenly pulled her into his body and held her tight. Exhaustion finally stopped her movements and her legs crumbled under her.

Stan gently eased them both to the kitchen floor, still holding her in his arms. Fiona could see the telephone close by, its digital face was blank and the unobtainable number was bleeping from the earpiece. Stan pushed the button to cancel it and she began to cry softly.

'I… I wouldn't have told them where I was. We would have been safe.'

'You wouldn't of had to. They could have just traced the call.'

Fiona gulped back the shock of his words. 'I'm so sorry,' she whispered.

She felt his breath by her ear. 'It's okay.'

'No. I am stupid. I put everyone at risk. But I… I was scared for my parents. I don't want them to suffer what happened to me.' Fiona croaked back a sob as fresh tears filled her eyes.

'They won't.'

She looked up into his face. His eyes were sparkling with amusement.

'What do you mean?' she sniffed.

He smiled. 'They are safe and so is your friend, Caroline and her family.'

Fiona had her mouth open but no words came out.

Stan continued, 'I realised, after our conversation, that your family and friends would be a worry for you, so I got some army buddies of mine to take care of it. That's what I've been doing today.'

Fiona just stared at him. 'They're all safe?'

Stan nodded.

An overwhelming feeling of gratitude filled her.

'Thank you, thank you so much.' She let the tears slip down her cheeks.

Stan wiped them away with the side of his finger. 'You're a brave woman to take me on like that.'

Fiona snorted and smiled, 'You only won because I'm not fully recovered yet.'

'Really?'

'Yep, really. But at the moment I need a lot of nurturing, so this is perfect.' She snuggled into his chest. 'If not a little hard on this floor.'

'Well, we'll have to do something about that, won't we?' Stan eased her away slightly and got up. Lifting her into his arms, he carried her back to her room and gently lowered her on to the bed.

Fiona kept her right arm around his neck so that he couldn't pull away. 'Stan, I'm sorry I didn't trust you.'

'You don't need to apologise. If I had told you what I was doing, then you would not have tried calling your parents.' He gently pulled her arm from him.

'Please stay with me for a while.' Fiona felt something inside she had never experienced before. A feeling that, for most of her life, had been hidden from her; a tenderness and warmth in her heart. Despite seeing Stan's dark and dangerous side, she instinctively knew she wanted to spend the rest of her life with him.

He sat on the bed and pushed back her hair. She could feel his hesitation, so she reached up and brought his face to her. She kissed him with a passion that surprised herself and when she drew away, she saw a sparkle in his eyes and then he was kissing her; a powerful and deep kiss that touched her heart.

CHAPTER SIXTEEN

Jane was in the baggage area of Windhoek airport, in Namibia, waiting for their cases. The journey had gone smoothly and she was stood next to Lola who was skipping from one foot to another in excitement.

'How long before we get to James's house?' Lola asked.

'About an hour. James is going to check to see if it's safe first.' Jane looked across to him. He was on his mobile and standing on the opposite side of the conveyor belt to where Mark was stood. Since they had left Glastonbury, James had only spoken one or two words to her and Mark the whole trip.

'He will be okay,' Lola said breaking into her thoughts.

Jane turned to her. 'Will he?'

Lola smiled. 'Yes, I will help him too.'

Jane turned away so Lola couldn't see her face. The guilt she was experiencing was growing and it was so hard to see poor James suffering.

Mark and James heaped the bags onto two trolleys and joined them. Lola gleefully jumped on top of the bags on James's trolley and let him push her out of the airport. Jane walked quietly alongside Mark.

'I don't think James is ever going to forgive me,' Mark said quietly.

'He will in time, Lola is working on him.'

Mark looked over to them. He smiled, 'She is something, isn't she?'

Jane watched too, capturing the graceful and serene movements Lola made as she leapt off the trolley when they reached the Jeep; the almost childlike innocence and playfulness Lola expressed as she began tickling James when he was trying to load her bags into the Jeep. 'She sure is,' Jane replied.

When they had caught up with them, Jane asked James, 'Is it safe at your house?'

James ignored Mark and moved to the side where Jane was standing. 'I've spoken to Kwasi and the men are gone. He and Aisha have cleaned out the house so it is fit for us.'

'And the lab stuff?' Mark asked, joining them.

'Don't know!' James grunted and got into the Jeep.

Mark shook his head and Jane took his hand, knowing exactly how he was feeling. Her many years of working with male managers who hated her, had toughened her up to being excluded, but it still didn't stop the pain that came with it. They got into the back, while Lola climbed in next to James.

The journey to James's house went quicker than Jane remembered it. Lola kept her nose pressed to the side window and screeched in delight every time she spotted a zebra or wildebeest. At one point she turned and grabbed Jane's arm in her excitement. Jane looked to where she was pointing and saw a lioness striding gracefully through the dry grass. Everything Lola saw seemed to bring amazement to her and she embraced it in a wonderment that was fresh and beautiful.

Kwasi and Aisha were waiting as they drove up, and while Mark helped Kwasi with the bags, James took Lola into the house. Jane took her rucksack to the bedroom, she felt depressed and the more she saw James with Lola, the more the depression deepened. She left the bedroom and slipped out the back door into James's garden. There was a bench, situated in a semi-circular area of flowers and bush, with a tree behind it offering shade. Jane sat on it, closed her eyes and deepened her breathing. It was time to reconnect with her guides.

The meadow shimmered with bright, rich, green grass and, the wild flowers, with their rainbow of colours, flashed in the sunlight. But, today, she did not appreciate it. Instead she walked through it all, blinded from its beauty. At the edge of the forest, no one was waiting for her. She looked around, but no one was there. So she called out, 'Three Wolves, I need to speak to you.' After a moment he appeared beside her.

'You are still troubled?'

Jane looked at him, her emotions bubbling up inside. 'I have done something terrible and I don't know what to do.'

Three Wolves indicated to her, to sit on the ground. 'Take off your shoes and put your feet on Mother Earth,' he instructed.

Jane did as he told her. 'Why am I doing this?'

'You have detached yourself from her.'

Jane sat for a few minutes, her bare feet flat on the ground, her toes crunching and squeezing the grass that slipped between them. It felt comforting, relaxing and almost like a forgotten pleasure. Her anxiety and gloom seemed to lift.

'Feeling better?' Three Wolves asked.

She smiled and wondered how he always knew what to do.

'Now tell me what you have done?' he said, sitting next to her.

Jane looked at him and even though her thoughts seemed sad, she felt supported in her emotions. 'I didn't heed Spirit Wind's advice. I have created something with devastating consequences,' she paused, feeling an ache in her chest. 'And if I create something else to stop my creation, then it will still end disastrously. I don't know what to do?'

Three Wolves sat quietly for a while. 'Your creation may not have been just yours.'

Jane looked at him puzzled.

He continued, 'We are all creators of our world. Our destiny is what we create.' He looked up to the sky as if something had drawn his attention. 'It is Lola who you must speak with.' He got up.

Jane got up with him, her mind still trying to understand what he had said. 'But…I…'

'Go, we will speak again.'

Jane moved away, disappointed; she thought her guides were there to help her, but all she felt now was rejection. She brought herself back to the bench and opened her eyes. She saw Lola approach and sit down next to her. She looked into Lola's soft, gentle gaze.

'I hope I didn't disturb you,' she whispered.

Jane looked down to the ground at her feet and the only lush grass in the garden. The depression and sadness was still stirring within her, so she slipped off her shoes and let her feet and toes feel the earth. Lola took hold of

Jane's left hand and held it in both of her hands. Jane began to cry. All the guilt and sorrow she had been carrying since Glastonbury overwhelming her. 'I'm… I'm so sorry, Lola. I didn't mean for this to happen.'

'It's okay,' Lola said sweetly.

'No it's not!' Jane said angrily, turning to her. 'I wished for someone to save us. Someone who would heal the crystals.'

'And your wish came true,' Lola said, smiling.

Jane pulled her hand away as more tears slipped down her face. 'You don't understand. I created you to save us without any thought of how that might affect you. And… now you might… die.' Jane covered her eyes with her hands and let the sobs come.

Lola said nothing but Jane could feel her presence and the loving energy that seemed to come from Lola's body touching her own. She finally pulled out a tissue from her trouser pocket and wiped her eyes. She looked up into Lola's serene face. 'I… I…' she shook her head, the words stuck in her throat.

Lola's soft, smooth hands cupped Jane's face and her voice was like silk. 'You did not create my destiny, lovely Jane. I was created for this very purpose and it is a destiny I choose to have.'

Jane tried to shake her head, but Lola's grip held her firm. 'Don't be sad, I am glad to be here.'

Jane reached up and took Lola's hands from her face. She held them and an amazing feeling of calmness began to fill her. 'You are so kind and gentle. I've never met anyone like you before.'

Lola smiled, 'You are seeing a part of you in me.'

Jane wanted to believe her, but at this moment all she could feel was regret. She took a deep breath and sighed.

'Do you know what I see in you?' Lola asked.

Jane sniffed back fresh tears, 'Sadness and guilt?'

'No. I see bravery, strength and courage to step up and admit you feel responsible. Now it's time to bring acceptance into your life.'

Jane looked at her as if she had said something outrageous. 'How can I do that when I know how this has affected people? Take James, he loves you so much and his grief will never stop him blaming Mark for what has happened. We have lost his friendship. I can't just accept that.'

Lola's face momentarily flashed with sadness, but she smiled again and said, 'What has happened, has happened for a reason. James will be all right. This is what you must accept.'

Jane took another deep breath. She was finding it really difficult to understand and accept what Lola was saying. Some part of her wanted to still suffer and hold on to the guilt, the regret, while another part of her wanted to believe Lola, and accept what had happened and move on.

'Now, no more sadness, lovely Jane. Let's go and play.'

Jane stared in astonishment as Lola slipped off her shoes, jumped up and began dancing after a butterfly; her delicate steps and the swirling of her white dress as her body twisted, was as graceful as a ballerina. Jane gripped the grass between her toes, her mind resisting Lola's invitations to follow her. Her rationale mind was telling her she was an adult and grown-ups don't do such things, but then a butterfly flittered past her head and the yearning of a childlike sense of excitement filled her. She leapt up on to her toes, swaying her body in rhythm with the butterfly's movements.

Lola clapped her hands, laughing, 'Come on, Jane, Come on.'

Jane giggled and danced her way in Lola's direction.

★★★

Several days had passed and Jane was sitting on the bench with Lola in the garden, making a ring of flowers. Her efforts were failing, as she was distracted with her thoughts about Mark. She was worried. He was spending all his waking hours in the lab, and the last time he spent so much time in close contact with the infected crystals, he hadn't been good. She was also worried about James. He seemed to be in two extremes when he was with Lola. One moment he was happy, but then he would get deeply depressed.

Lola tapped her hand. 'Look how pretty this is,' she said, holding up her flower ring.

'Better job than mine,' Jane muttered, holding up a rather ragged mess of flower heads.

Lola looked at it and pointed to Jane's head. 'Your thoughts are not here. Only think about this time and place.'

Jane shook her head. All she seemed to have in her mind were negative thoughts, which kept on reminding her that what she was doing was wasting time. That she should be worrying all the time, not enjoying herself. Yet it was so difficult to be sad in Lola's presence. Peace and stillness seemed to surround her, and joy and laughter always found their way into whatever they were doing.

'Okay, just watch this,' Jane joked, and focussing on the moment, she completed a fresh ring of flowers that were perfect.

Lola placed the ring she'd made on top of Jane's head. 'You are a Lady of Avalon, now.'

Jane did the same with her ring, noticing that the air around Lola's head seemed to sparkle with a life force of its own. A halo of sunlight appeared and flowed down onto Lola's head. Jane gasped.

Lola giggled, 'You have a magic touch.'

Jane looked at her joyful face, 'Lola, will you tell me about your life?'

Lola took both of Jane's hands. 'It will be an honour. But maybe you would like to experience it?'

'Experience it? What do you mean?'

'If you are agreeable, I have the ability to connect with you.'

Jane held back, but seeing the glow in Lola's eyes, she nodded.

Immediately Jane felt herself being drawn into another world. She was no longer in Africa but in a hospital maternity ward somewhere in England. She was a baby being handed to a young woman. Jane could see the joy and love in the woman's soft brown eyes as she cradled her. Somehow Jane could feel the love and happiness in this woman's heart. Then Jane saw a man's head come into view, his sparkling grey eyes were watery and in them she felt how proud and grateful he was. Amazingly, Jane wasn't picking up the physical aspects of Lola's foster parents just their emotions and feelings.

The next moment, Jane was at junior school, in the playground. She was dancing along the line markings on the ground and the other girls were behind her doing the same. Jane could pick up their fun and joy. Then she was sat next to another girl who was crying and Jane could feel her sadness. When the girl stopped crying Jane took her hand to hold it. Love and compassion seemed to flow between their hands and the girl's face soon lifted and she smiled.

Finally Jane was Lola as a grown woman in a crystal shop. The crystals seemed to be speaking to her and each time she held one, a wonderful feeling entered her body. Jane felt it was like having pure energy light up the inside of her. In response the crystals glowed brighter.

Jane felt Lola let go of her hands. She took a deep breath to bring her back to the present. 'Wow! That's amazing, Lola. You feel everyone's emotions.'

'Yes, it's a beautiful gift.'

'But what about the negative ones, like anger? You were quite upset, in Glastonbury, when James got annoyed with Mark.'

Lola nodded. 'I find them hard to be around. They hurt like you experience pain.'

Jane was glad Lola hadn't shared that with her. 'Are your foster mum and dad still alive?'

'No, they passed on when I left school. Yours?'

Jane felt a twinge of sadness touch her heart, remembering her own parents' sudden and untimely death. She felt Lola touch her chest and immediately the sadness lifted.

'Don't be sad for your parents' death, Jane. We all have a path to follow in this lifetime and when it is time, we return home. My parents gave me a wonderful experience of home and family life and for that I will always be grateful to them.'

'How do you cope with the grief?' Jane asked.

'I let out my emotions to my stone brothers and sisters and then I remember the wonderful times and love my parents gave me and I know that these gifts, that were part of them, are now in me,' she paused and when Jane made eye contact with her, she said, 'Don't remember them with sadness, remember them with love and gratitude.'

Jane nodded, knowing she needed to do some work to forgive them first for leaving her alone and the anger at herself for letting it happen. 'I think I shall have to speak to the stones.'

Lola smiled and handed her a stone. 'They love helping us. Just blow your emotions in and give them back to the Earth. Then think about the good things your parents did for you and hold that in your heart.'

Jane took the stone just as a shadow of a figure fell over them. She looked up to see James, his face was taught and there were deep furrows across his brow. 'What is it?' she asked, putting the stone in her pocket.

Lola shifted along the bench to make room for him.

'It's…awful…' James said, slumping down hard between them.

He looked at Lola and Jane saw his face lighten. The

tension in his body immediately disappeared when Lola placed her hand on his chest.

'You look lovely,' he said in a whisper. 'So lovely.'

'James?' Jane called him, trying to bring him back to why he had come. 'What was it you were going to say?'

James turned to her and for a moment he seemed lost in an emotion. If Jane didn't know him better, she would have believed he had been taking some kind of drug, as his eyes were glazed and his face soft, almost absent in thought. She looked at Lola. Yes, James was high, high on his love for Lola.

'What's awful?' she persisted.

James blinked himself back to reality, remembering what he had come to tell them. 'The mine…it's the mine. All the crystals are black.' He gulped before turning to Lola. 'I think they're all dead.'

Jane saw the light around Lola fade; her face went even paler and her smile faded. 'My friends are dead?' Her voice was so low Jane could hardly hear her. Lola took James's hand, 'We must do something, please.'

Jane looked on as James brought Lola's hand to his lips and kissed it. 'I don't know what we can do,' he said sadly. 'Mark is the one…' He stopped speaking and Jane saw Mark approaching them, his face was flushed and he was smiling. In his hand he held a large, nearly two feet long, glowing clear crystal that was pointed at both ends.

Jane got up quickly, 'You did it?' she shouted.

Mark's smile widened. 'This is a master crystal, a crystal with a pure symmetry; unlike anything I've created or seen before. It's lattice is filled with atoms that hold positive energy and reject negativity.'

Lola stood up, her eyes focused on the crystal, her face filled with wonderment. 'May I touch it?' she asked, gently stretching out her left hand.

Mark passed the crystal to her and the instant she touched it, the glow turned into a flash of light that grew brighter and brighter. Lola began to laugh, 'It's singing to me, oh my, such a beautiful melody of love and gratitude.'

Mark nodded. 'I heard it too.'

'Then this will work by itself?' James asked, hope in his voice.

Jane saw a slight hesitation in Mark's face before he said, 'It works on crystals smaller than itself, clearing them completely, but it's not strong enough to do larger ones.'

'Then we'll build a bigger one!' James declared.

Mark didn't speak.

'You can build a bigger one, can't you?' James asked tentatively.

'The size isn't what makes it stronger,' Mark said, looking at Lola. 'It's the energy that's put into it.'

Jane could see the light from the crystal in Lola's hand was much stronger now and when Lola laughed, it got bigger.

'Let's test it now,' Lola said, and began to walk quickly towards the house.

James went after her. 'Let's not rush things,' he said nervously.

Lola stopped and turned to him. 'My crystal friends are dying, it's time to stop it.'

James's head dropped slightly. Lola held out her hand and said, 'I need your love, James, to do this.' He nodded and took her hand.

Jane followed them into the lab room and moved to a corner where she could see what was happening but be out of the way. Mark put on protective gloves and positioned several large crystals on the workbench which had different levels of infection. He beckoned Lola forward. Jane noticed that James still held her hand and was reluctant to let go.

Lola turned to him and smiled. 'It's okay. These are only little ones.'

James quickly kissed her lips and stepped back.

Jane took hold of his hand and he glanced at her. His face was drawn and Jane could see fear in his eyes. He squeezed her hand and turned back to watch.

Mark said to Lola, 'Place the master crystal tip on this smaller infected one.'

Lola did as he instructed and when the point made contact, the small crystal began to glow. The light seemed to flow from the master crystal and in seconds the dark virus was extinguished.

Lola grinned, 'It's healed.' She moved to the next crystal and again the virus was gone in seconds. As she did each one, her joy was growing, but when she reached the last one, the largest at nearly a foot and a half long, she hesitated. 'This one is dead?' she asked.

Mark nodded. 'It has no vibration, so I don't know if you can do anything once the crystal has gone completely black.'

Lola closed her eyes and brought the master crystal to her heart. The room went quiet and still. She opened her eyes and her smile broadened as she kissed the crystal.

'What is it, Lola?' Jane called to her.

'I have been told that once the virus is gone, new energy will return and the crystal will be stronger than before.' Lola placed the point of the master crystal on the completely black one. The light stream between the two crystals seemed to sparkle and crackle as it grew stronger.

At first Jane could see no change, but then the darkness in the crystal started to lighten to a grey. Soon after, the point of the dark crystal began to glow brightly and a light moved down the crystal pushing and dissolving the virus. When the light reached the base of the crystal, the virus had completely gone.

'YES!' Mark shouted punching the air and immediately hugging Lola.

'We did it,' she laughed, handing back the master crystal and turning into the arms of James. They hugged and kissed.

Jane could feel the relief spread throughout the room. She hugged herself, holding back her emotions. Dare she believe that this would work? Could she risk letting herself enjoy this moment? The next thing she knew, Mark was stood in front of her. He pulled her into his arms.

'Thank you for believing in me,' he whispered in her ear.

Jane hugged him, 'Will this really work?' she asked tentatively, not wanting to sound too negative, but thinking back to what Mark had said earlier about Lola not being strong enough.

He drew back and kissed her forehead. 'It's a start. We have to test the really large crystals yet.'

Jane caught the faint tone of caution in his voice.

James turned to them, 'You want Lola to go to the mine?'

Mark nodded. 'But first, I want to test the vibrations of these healed ones.' He turned to Lola. 'You may need to bring more of your energy into the master crystal when we tackle the ones at the mine.'

Lola smiled, 'It will be no trouble, I can draw more if James is with me.'

'Okay then, everyone out, I have work to do,' Mark shuffled them all towards the door. 'This afternoon we'll go to the mine.'

CHAPTER SEVENTEEN

Jane entered the lounge after spending a couple of hours in the garden. James and Lola were sitting on the sofa, their bodies so close that even a credit card would have trouble slipping between them. It was obvious from the way they looked at and touched each other they didn't want to be disturbed.

Jane tried to stop the dull, empty feeling from sinking into her stomach, but it was determined to anchor itself. She slipped quietly past one of the armchairs hoping not to disturb them, but James spotted her.

'Why so sad, Jane?' he asked, sitting forward. 'Mark's resolved the problem and Lola is safe.'

Jane glanced at Lola and their eyes met briefly before Jane looked away.

'Jane is sad because she believes she created me to heal the crystals and she feels responsible for anything that happens to me,' Lola said gently.

'Rubbish! Anyway, nothing is going to happen to you,' James said, touching Lola's face.

Jane went to speak, but Lola spoke first, 'My sweetest love, there is still a risk. I don't have the energy to clear all the infected crystals. There are too many.'

'But...'

Lola stopped James from speaking with a finger on his lips. 'Mark will have to call up the energy of the universe to help me.'

'So?' James didn't want to listen. Jane could see his

resistance as his body stiffened.

'So, I will not survive. The energy of the universe will spread the healing, but to bring balance, it takes energy from its surroundings and it will completely absorb me.'

James shook his head violently. 'No it may not! Lola, it may not!' he cried desperately.

Jane sniffed back the tears as she watched James fight to hold back his.

'I… I thought Mark had found a safe solution,' he stammered.

Lola took his face in her hands and kissed him softly. She said, 'He has. He's made it safe for me to transmit my energy to the crystals. I won't become infected, but I cannot protect myself from the energy of the universe. It has to go through me.'

'I don't understand why you have to die.'

Lola snuggled closer to him. 'I won't be dead, I will have transformed into something else. You will see me in every crystal, in every rock.'

Tears were flowing down James's face.

'Don't be sad, my love. You will feel me and I will be with you, always.' Lola smiled. 'Think of this as being the greatest journey of my life, please don't be angry or upset. I want this, and I want your love to be with me, not your sadness.'

Jane took out a tissue from her trousers and wiped away her own tears. Even though she felt sad, she also felt a strange happiness that seemed to be coming from her heart. A feeling of wonderment seemed to be lifting her spirit and when she looked over to James, she could see it happening to him too.

At that moment, Mark entered the room; he stopped for a moment, sensing the atmosphere.

James got up when he saw him and Mark unconsciously took a step back.

'What are the results?' James asked stiffly.

Mark cleared his throat before answering. 'Good. All crystals are virus free and vibrating at an incredible level.'

'But you can't save my Lola,' James said flatly.

Mark shook his head guiltily, his body tensing ready for James's reaction. 'I can't find a way. I'm so sorry.'

James gave a big sigh and stepped forward. Mark stepped back further and flinched as James's hands fell on to his shoulders. 'Thank you for trying,' he said softly. Without saying another word, he returned to the sofa and sat down next to Lola.

Mark stood rigid in shock. Jane could see confusion on his face.

'Do we need to go to the mine?' James asked, pushing back Lola's red hair from her face. 'If Lola needs the universal energy to do this, why don't we just go straight to Ferrand's mine?'

Jane looked at James in disbelief. 'Now?' she quizzed him.

James shook his head. 'I would like some more time with Lola before we do this.' He looked at Lola. 'Have we time?'

Lola smiled, her hand resting on his chest over his heart. 'We have as much time as you need.'

★★★

Mark and Jane lay in bed snuggled in each other's arms. Jane could sense something was wrong for Mark had gone quiet. 'What's bothering you?' she asked softly.

'It's been a week since I perfected the master crystal and tomorrow we go to Ferrand's mine.' He paused as if trying to find the right words. He finally said, 'I don't know if I can do this.'

Jane raised her head and looked at him. 'Why?'

'Because if it was you, instead of Lola, I don't think I could bear to lose you.'

Jane had to admit that very thought had been on her mind too. 'It's a hard decision, yes, but if you don't do it, we all die anyway.'

She heard Mark moan. 'I'd be happier if you weren't there. I want you to stay here.'

'What's wrong?' She sat up worried.

'Nothing.' Mark diverted his gaze.

'Nothing, my arse, tell me.'

Mark took a deep breath. 'I don't know what will happen when the energy is created. It's going to be bigger than anything I have done before and it could destroy us all.' His body relaxed as if, having finally said it, it removed the burden he had been carrying.

'You think it's going to be that powerful?'

'I don't know, I just think that to do what it needs to do, it has to be.'

Jane touched his face and waited until his eyes focused on her. 'If we are going to die, then I want to die with you.' He made to speak but she stopped him. 'You can't bear to lose me and I can't live without you. I want us to be together, no matter what happens.' She kissed him and he pulled her to him, returning her kiss with urgency. His lips moved down her neck, tasting her skin with his tongue. Gently he moved on top of her, holding her face in his hands and kissing her long and hard. Jane so much wanted this moment to last. Her need for him was overpowering, bursting uncontrollably out of her body as her nails dug into his skin and her body twisted in pleasure at his touch. They made love, joined in unison as one. A moment of pure ecstasy that felt like it lasted a lifetime.

★★★

The next morning Jane noticed that no one but Lola touched their breakfast. Her own stomach was churning and her whole body felt uneasy. James looked tired, as if he hadn't slept, whereas Lola looked bright and happy. Mark was flicking through his notebook, reading a bit, then turning more pages. He looked nervous. 'Is everything ready?' Jane asked in a whisper, which seemed loud in the uncannily quiet room.

'Yes, yes. Just checking my notes on the process.' Mark looked at James. 'I can't tell you what to expect as I don't know myself.'

James nodded gravely.

Mark continued, 'But you need to know that the force of this energy could kill us all, not just Lola.'

Jane saw James's face lighten as if this was good news. He became suddenly serious. 'We're all going to die now.'

Mark shook his head sadly. 'I don't know, but yes, it's possible, unless you stay here.'

James gave a cough and in his most English accent he

said, 'My dear fellow, what an absurd suggestion. For King and Country.' He raised his orange juice glass.

Jane stared at him.

His face broke into a smile and he began to laugh. *Was this some kind of madness?* she thought. Mark's face must have reflected the same thought for James quickly said, 'It's okay, I've made my peace with this. I'm just trying to break up the tension in here.'

Mark took a deep breath. 'Not exactly a good way to do it, James,' he said quietly.

The atmosphere in the room changed and there was a sense of relief. Jane looked at Lola and knew this beautiful woman had brought something special to them all.

Lola smiled at her and said, 'It's time to go.'

Everyone seemed to hesitate, as if not doing anything would prevent it happening, but Lola got up. She was filled with excitement as if she was going on a holiday or going to some special celebration. Jane found it hard to conjure up those same feelings, but she got up too.

The journey to Ferrand's mine didn't seem to take as long as Jane remembered the last time they went there. Lola was sat with Jane in the back and didn't stop talking all the way. She embraced the beauty of the land, pointing out to Jane the colours and shapes. The beautiful clear blue sky and the fluffy white clouds. Jane tried to see them as Lola did, but it was difficult to override the feeling of doom, the closer they got to the mine.

Lola sat back against the seat, breathless. She took Jane's hand. 'I want you to know why I'm so happy.' She paused for a moment, closing her eyes as if savouring something really pleasurable. 'Remember you experienced a part of my life, well, what you didn't experience is the feeling I have always had. Hmm, how can I describe it to you? You know when something happens and it excites you and you can't wait to do it?'

Jane nodded.

'Well, this is it. I'm going to become what I've been created to do and it's wonderful.'

Jane squeezed Lola's hand. She couldn't find any words to say.

'And you know what the best part has been?' Lola said.

'What?' Jane croaked.

'I've experienced so much love.'

Jane swallowed hard. 'That's wonderful, Lola.'

The Jeep pulled up at the end of the track, close to the destroyed shacks and tents of the mine. Jane looked out and noticed everything was quite dark even though the sun was nearly overhead. 'Is it safe?' she asked Mark.

James opened the door and looked at the ground. 'I've never seen anything like this before. Could the virus have spread on the surface?'

Mark opened his door. 'I don't know, but if it has we shouldn't touch it.' He looked over to what was left of the shacks and pointed to one that was partly still standing. 'Pull up over there and we can step out from the Jeep to the steps. I need to unpack the crystal before we drive closer to the drill hole.'

James and Mark closed their doors and James drove them to the shack. He got out onto the step and helped Jane and Lola climb out from the back. Mark crawled over the seats to the back and retrieved the box the crystal was stored in.

Jane walked into the half-demolished shack. Tables and chairs had been smashed and part of the rear wall had been blown away. Bits of paper littered the floor. *Stan has done a thorough job destroying this place,* she thought. She moved forward and looked out of the broken rear wall. Crystal fragments lay scattered on the ground and they were all black. She gasped and stepped back into someone behind her. It was Mark.

'No one touch the ground,' he shouted and moved his gaze to the shack floor. 'And keep away from the dark bits in the corners.'

Jane looked into his face, seeing the shock and worry in his expression. 'Can we still do this?' she asked.

Mark opened his box and pulled out his master crystal. 'I don't know,' he answered softly. The crystal was glowing brightly and lit up the interior of the shack like a fluorescent light. 'This master crystal should generate enough energy with…'

'MARK!' James sudden yell made them turn round. He was pointing to something above Lola's head on the left-hand wall. It was a video camera.

'Is it working?' Mark asked anxiously moving towards it.

James nodded pointing to the little red flashing light.

'DAMN!' Mark pushed the crystal into Jane's hands and, picking up a piece of table leg, he smashed the camera to bits.

'What does this mean?' Jane asked, feeling suddenly vulnerable.

Mark turned to her. 'It means that Ferrand knows we're here and he knows I have this.' He pointed to the crystal she was holding. 'We don't have much time and we haven't worked out how we are going to get to the drill hole without becoming infected.'

'Hmm, yes we have,' Lola said quietly, from the corner by the door. She pointed to her feet.

Lola was standing in the corner of the shack where Mark had spotted dark bits on the floor. The darkness was gone.

'You think I have enough resistance to it to create a clear area?'

Mark looked at her and then the area outside. He seemed to be pondering something. 'No.'

'Why?' James asked.

Mark turned to him. 'We can't risk Lola being infected. If she becomes infected and we use the energy it will make things worse.' He moved to Lola and pulled her away from the corner. 'Do you feel anything negative?'

She smiled. 'No. I'm good.'

He groaned. 'I can't even test you, to check.'

Jane saw something shiny catching the light in the corner. 'Mark, look.' She pointed to it.

He bent down and said, 'Lola, you beauty. You stood on a crystal fragment?'

She nodded.

'You didn't have direct contact?'

She shook her head.

Mark kissed her on her cheek and moved back to the box. He pulled out the crystal pieces Lola had healed in the lab. 'We can use these to create a safe pathway. Let's go.'

They got back into the Jeep and drove to where the drill hole had been. All the equipment had been blown up and the only thing left was a hole of rubble with black crystal shards pointing out of it.

Mark gave them each a healed crystal. 'Place this on the floor and stand on it. Wait until the darkness clears around it before moving it on. Try not to stand on the ground for too long as the crystal will only be able to clear the top surface for a short time.'

Lola gently placed her crystal to the ground and got out on to it. Within minutes the area around it cleared. She stepped off and moved the crystal further up towards the drill hole.

Jane placed her crystal in the same spot as Lola had placed hers and was able to step on the path spots Lola had left without fully using her own crystal. She followed Lola. James followed her and finally Mark.

When they reached the drill hole Mark noticed the debris. 'I'll have to clear the hole so that the master crystal can connect directly to the Vogel one beneath. I hope it hasn't been too badly damaged.'

Lola took his crystal and her own, and held them to her heart before placing them either side of the hole. Minutes later, the rocks and crystal shards had lost the darkness and it was safe for Mark to clear it away.

Jane watched him work, her stomach twisting and cramping with anxiety. She had tried to prepare herself for this, but the fear of doing it, and also, of not doing it, made her feel sick. Every part of her wanted to run away and hide, to delude herself into thinking she would be okay and that this was nothing, or something someone else could deal with. Being here and experiencing the whole thing, was terrifying.

She heard Mark gasp and instinctively she moved

forward. The rocks and broken crystal bits had been removed to reveal the tip of the Vogel crystal and it was like looking into a black hole. Mark began to groan. James leapt forward, dragging him back. Mark's hands and face were etched with dark veins.

'NO!' Jane cried, moving James away, but Lola got in before her. She put the master crystal she was holding across Mark's chest and placed her hands over it. It took only seconds before Mark's appearance returned to normal.

'Thank you,' he said, breathing in deeply. Lola smiled and moved away so Jane could get closer. 'I'm okay,' he responded, to Jane's anxious look. 'But we need to hurry.' He got up.

'It's time to say our goodbyes,' Lola said quietly. 'And for me to give you each a gift.' She moved to Mark first. 'You still have a powerful journey to undertake. You can do it. Thank you for doing this for me.'

Mark dropped his head. 'For killing you?'

Lola kissed his cheek. 'No, for giving me my destiny. Here is my gift to you.'

Jane saw Lola place her hand on his chest over his heart and something seemed to enter his body. It created a glow on his skin and she saw Mark smile.

Lola moved to her next. Jane could feel the tears in her eyes and a heaviness in her chest.

'Lovely Jane, you have an inner strength that guides you well. I will treasure the time we have enjoyed together. Thank you for finding me.'

Tears were flowing down Jane's face now, but she knew what she wanted to say. 'You are amazing. So kind and gentle. I will miss you.'

Lola smiled, 'I am but a reflection of you. Here is my gift to you.'

Lola placed her hand over Jane's heart and it was like a warm flow of energy entering her body. It seemed to grow stronger, gently soothing the weight in her chest, washing away the fear in her belly and lifting her spirit so that she felt light and free. Jane smiled and then laughed. She hugged Lola and whispered, 'Let's play again sometime.'

Lola smiled and nodded her head.

Jane watched her move to James. She felt no sadness in her body as she watched Lola and James hug and kiss, for she knew that James and Lola would be okay.

Lola gently pulled away from James and held both hands to his heart. 'You have shown me so much love and kindness. There are no words to describe how I feel.'

James touched her pale skin. 'You are so beautiful, my Lady of Avalon. Everything you say is like nectar to my ears. Your touch is healing to my heart.'

Lola smiled even more. 'For you I give everything. You have my heart.' She kissed him again and stepped back. 'It's time.'

Jane and James made their way back along the clear path to stand by the Jeep. They could still see and hear what was happening, but were far enough away so as not to get in the way.

Mark gave Lola the master crystal and she held it to her heart. It began to glow brighter until its light seemed as strong as the sun. She kneeled at the drill hole and placed the crystal on to the tip of the Vogel. The light from the master crystal began to penetrate the Vogel, pushing back the virus.

'Tell me when the Vogel is free of the virus,' Mark yelled, as he searched in his trouser pocket for something.

Jane saw him pull out a crystal pyramid made from three crystal points joined together to form the shape. She recognised it as the gift Mark had been given from Michael, when he had saved the old man from the cliff fall. She hadn't realised he still had it.

He placed it on the ground and knelt over it. 'How's it coming?' he asked Lola.

Lola seemed to be struggling to hold onto the master crystal for the light was so intense and it was expanding around her. 'It's stuck right at the end.'

Jane felt James move forward. She grabbed his arm pulling him back. 'You can't do anything, just send her your love.' She gripped his hand.

Lola looked towards them and smiled. She seemed to sense what they were doing. She turned back to the master crystal and began to sing. The tone was soothing and sweeter than any bird song; its sound stronger than storm force winds. It created a vibration in the master crystal that caused the light to get even brighter. Its radiance surrounded Lola totally now and Jane could hardly see her body through the glow. Still Lola sang, a lovely sound Jane would remember and feel forever.

'We are ready,' Lola said and continued singing.

Jane heard Mark start to chant words she didn't understand. He raised his hands to the sky, feeling with his fingers. Jane saw what was like a heat wave resting on his fingertips. When he moved his hands higher to cup it, there were sparks of energy, like twinkling stars, forming in an invisible bowl between his hands. The sparks began to merge and Jane could see a spot of light in the centre of his hands. It started to grow until the light filled the whole space between his hands. He brought it down towards his chest. It was still growing and he opened his hands further to create a space a foot wide. The energy quickly filled it, so he moved his hands out even further.

Jane could see he was struggling to hold it, as it began to slip between his fingers. She glanced at Lola who was now almost obscured from view. The light around her was like looking at the centre of the sun and Jane had to shield her eyes. She could still hear Lola singing.

Then suddenly a glistening, transparent hand came out of the light and Mark placed the energy ball on to it. The instant Lola's hand brought the ball of energy into the light there was a blinding flash.

Jane covered her eyes. Seconds later, she heard a whoosh sound and was lifted off her feet. She was flying above the Jeep and right across the mine, her journey ending as she hit something hard and fell to the floor. For a long time she lay struggling to find her breath, her body heaving and gasping for the air it needed. Underneath her she felt the ground tremble. She was helpless, her body locked in a struggle to get air.

The shaking ground bounced her body a few times, then stopped. Gradually her body calmed and she was able to breath properly. Gently she looked up. The force of what happened had sent her as far as the shacks, a good distance from the drill hole. James was laid about ten feet away from her to the right. He was still, but breathing. The Jeep was on its side next to him.

She quickly looked for Mark and Lola. The drill hole

was glowing and the area around it was bright but slowly fading to normal light. Lola was nowhere to be seen; neither was Mark. With no regard to any injuries she may have suffered, Jane sat up. Her eyes scanned the area of the hole, nothing. She looked round the mine edges and saw a heap of what looked like clothes.

'MARK!' she screamed and, getting to her feet, she staggered over to where he lay on his side. She fell to her knees and gently turned him on to his back. There was no rise or fall to indicate breathing and putting her ear to his chest she could just hear a faint heart beat. Quickly she pushed back his head, held his mouth closed and blew air into his nose two, then three times. She stopped and looked at him for signs he was breathing on his own. 'Please, please, Mark,' she cried pulling his body towards her.

He suddenly gasped and heaved in a breath. Her tears fell on his face and he opened his eyes. 'Lola?' he asked. Jane shook her head. He closed his eyes for a second as if the news was too much to bear. They heard James before they saw him.

'LOLA, LOLA!' he yelled as he made his way up to the drill hole. 'My Lola,' he sobbed, falling to his knees by the hole.

Jane gripped Mark's hand. She knew exactly how James was feeling and she couldn't bear to hear his cries. Mark got up and helped Jane to her feet. Amazingly they were unhurt. They walked up to the drill hole to James who was mumbling and holding something to his chest.

Mark inspected the land and the Vogel. 'It looks clear,' he said relieved.

The ground began to shake around their feet and Jane

leapt back. Mark grabbed James, pulling him further away from the hole. The ground seemed to split apart, like a earthquake and almost immediately move together again, forcing the crystals to collapse into the hole, sealing itself under a mound of earth.

James got to his feet and stared at them. He was smiling. Jane was shocked but also curious. 'What is it?'

He pulled his hands away from his chest and opened them. Nestling in his palms was the remains of the master crystal, which had morphed into the shape of a heart. It was radiating a beautiful rainbow of light.

'Lola said I have her heart,' James said. 'She is here, feel it.'

Jane tentatively touched the heart with her fingers. It was amazing; she could feel Lola's energy. Her gentleness and love were radiating out of the crystal as if she was there in person. 'She is here, that's wonderful,' Jane beamed.

Mark picked up a stone from the ground and said, 'She's here too.'

Jane took the stone and the feelings were still there though not as strong. 'Have we really done it?'

Mark put his arm around her. 'I want to do some test drills and check out James's mine, but I think we did.' He looked over her shoulder and left her to pick up something from the ground. It was his crystal pyramid.

'I saw you with that, what did it do?'

Mark smiled. 'I had a message from my guide last night in a dream. He told me to use it, but I don't know what it did.' He popped it into his pocket.

James turned to them and, pointing to the Jeep, he

said, 'I think I'll need a hand with pushing our transport back on its wheels.'

'How do you know it'll work?' Jane asked.

'Lola told me,' he said, kissing the crystal.

Any other time Jane would have said he was mad, but after this how could she not believe totally.

As they walked back to the Jeep, James said to Mark, 'We need to get you and Jane away from here. Where do you think you'll go?'

Mark looked at Jane and gave her a hug. 'I think it's time to stop running, don't you?'

Jane couldn't believe she was hearing this. Something in Mark had changed, *in fact*, she thought, *we have all been changed in some way.* 'What are you going to do?' she asked cautiously.

'Ferrand knows about the master crystal, he'll not stop until he gets it. I don't want anyone else to get hurt,' he paused then said, 'I'm going to find my parents and my children. I need to make sure they're safe. Then I'm going to confront Ferrand.'

'But... but you can't. Once he has this power, he'll kill you.' Jane could feel the fear returning.

Mark kissed her gently on the forehead. 'It's time to put an end to this.'

'Well I don't know about you two, but I've had enough adventure to last me a lifetime.' James smiled, 'But I know just the man to help you.'